Collier's Junior Classics

1 Let's Read Together
2 Animal Tales and Fables
3 Once Upon a Time
4 Long Ago and Far Away
5 In the Family Circle
6 School and Beyond
7 The Best of Friends
8 Myths and Legends
9 Magic and Mystery
10 Learning and Growing
11 Adventures in the Wild
12 Home and Away
13 Many Roads to Glory
14 Journeys to Discovery
15 On the High Seas
16 A Reader's Treasury

COLLIER'S JUNIOR CLASSICS

VOLUME 15

On the High Seas

P. F. COLLIER, INC.

NEW YORK TORONTO SYDNEY

Cover illustration by Arvis Stewart

On the High Seas

Printed in the United States of America

P. F. Collier, Inc.
866 Third Avenue
New York, N.Y. 10022

P. F. Collier & Son Ltd.
7 Taymall Avenue
Etobicoke, Ontario
Canada M8Z 6A5

INTRODUCTION

A love of reading is one of the most valuable gifts parents can give their children. The literary treasures assembled in the 16-volume *Collier's Junior Classics*, all chosen by experts, offer parents the perfect resource for instilling the wonder of words and images in children of any age while imparting a strong sense of fundamental values. Through the years, parents will have the joy of watching children turn to *Collier's Junior Classics* again and again — to master reading skills, gain understanding of the world, and explore the infinite possibilities of the imagination. *Collier's Junior Classics* is sure to become one of the most valuable components of the Collier's Home Learning Center.

Collier's Junior Classics assembles masterpieces of literature from around the world, starting with nursery rhymes and culminating in extracts from great novels that students will encounter in high school and later on. Material presented progresses from easy to more challenging, both within each volume and across the set as a whole. This structure allows children to build up their skills as they read through one book and then go on to the next. It also permits readers at various levels to find interesting, accessible material in each volume.

The individual volumes of *Collier's Junior Classics* have themes to match a variety of interests — magic, family, friendship, school, and seafaring, for example. Selections within each volume offer a range of subjects and settings. Popular subjects recur throughout the set, so that a reader who loved "The Good Horse Kristie" (Volume 1) can go on to read about the winged horse Pegasus (Volume 8), "Pony Penning Day" (Volume 11), and "Black Beauty" (Volume 12).

Collier's Junior Classics grows with its readers. Preschoolers will treasure the first volumes, sharing a special closeness with the adults who read aloud to them. Then, as the children start learning to read, they will thrill all over again to discover for themselves the Velveteen Rabbit, the crafty Puss in Boots, and all the other characters in these beloved stories and rhymes.

Later volumes give young readers a head start in learning about the life and literature of different cultures. Reading will bring children both enjoyment and a sense of accomplishment as they savor the timeless charm of *Alice's Adventures in Wonderland* or whitewash the fence with Tom Sawyer. They will meet great figures of the past — Marie Curie, Louis Armstrong, and Mohandas Gandhi, to name a few — as well as the gods and heroes of ancient myths and legends. They will visit the little house on the Kansas prairie, Heidi's grandparents high in the Swiss Alps, and the Yorkshire village to which Lassie came home, among many other people and places.

The final volumes of *Collier's Junior Classics* round out the series. By now reading has become an adventure in itself, and there is plenty of adventure to be found here. Readers will shudder at the villainy of pirate Long John Silver and watch helplessly as Don Quixote tilts at windmills. Learning about medieval chivalry from *The Merry Adventures of Robin Hood* and *Ivanhoe*, seeing human nature revealed through Jane Austen's and Charles Dickens's unforgettable characters, they will gain an appreciation of what makes these works true classics — a perfect foundation for learning and for life.

CONTENTS

1 The Apple Barrel
by ROBERT LOUIS STEVENSON

18 Call It Courage
by ARMSTRONG SPERRY

29 The Gold Bug
by EDGAR ALLAN POE

68 The Devil Fish
by JULES VERNE

77 Gulliver's Voyage to Lilliput
by JONATHAN SWIFT

133 The Swiss Family Robinson
by JOHANN WYSS

143 Friday's Rescue
by DANIEL DEFOE

153 Captains Courageous
by RUDYARD KIPLING

183 ACKNOWLEDGMENTS

The Apple Barrel

BY ROBERT LOUIS STEVENSON

Illustrations by Emil Weiss

In Treasure Island, one of the most thrilling adventure stories ever written, young Jim Hawkins, Squire Trelawney, and Dr. Livesey engage in a struggle to the death with murderous pirates. Fortunately, Jim overheard Long John Silver, Black Dog, and their henchmen plotting mutiny and the theft of the treasure buried by the notorious Captain Flint.

ALL that night we were in a great bustle getting things stowed in their place, and boatfuls of the squire's friends, Mr. Blandly and the like, coming off to wish him a good voyage and a safe return. We never had a night at the "Admiral Benbow" when I had half the work; and I was dog-tired when, a little before dawn, the boatswain sounded his pipe, and the crew began to man the capstan-bars. I might have been twice as weary, yet I would not have left the deck; all was so new and interesting to me—the brief commands, the shrill note of the whistle, the men bustling to their places in the glimmer of the ship's lanterns.

"Now, Barbecue, tip us a stave," cried one voice.

"The old one," cried another.

"Ay, ay, mates," said Long John, who was standing by, with his crutch under his arm, and at once broke out in the air and words I knew so well—

"Fifteen men on the dead man's chest"—

And then the whole crew bore chorus—

"Yo-ho-ho, and a bottle of rum!"

From *Treasure Island,* by Robert Louis Stevenson.

And at the third "ho!" drove the bars before them with a will.

Even at that exciting moment it carried me back to the old "Admiral Benbow" in a second; and I seemed to hear the voice of the captain piping in the chorus. But soon the anchor was short up; soon it was hanging dripping at the bows; soon the sails began to draw, and the land and shipping to flit by on either side; and before I could lie down to snatch an hour of slumber the *Hispaniola* had begun her voyage to the Isle of Treasure.

I am not going to relate that voyage in detail. It was fairly prosperous. The ship proved to be a good ship, the crew were capable seamen, and the captain thoroughly understood his business. But before we came the length of Treasure Island, two or three things had happened which require to be known.

Mr. Arrow, first of all, turned out even worse than the captain had feared. He had no command among the men, and people did what they pleased with him. But that was by no means the worst of it; for after a day or two at sea he began to appear on deck with hazy eye, red cheeks, stuttering tongue, and other marks of drunkenness. Time after time he was ordered below in disgrace. Sometimes he fell and cut himself; sometimes he lay all day long in his little bunk at one side of the companion;

sometimes for a day or two he would be almost sober and attend to his work at least passably.

In the meantime, we could never make out where he got the drink. That was the ship's mystery. Watch him as we pleased, we could do nothing to solve it; and when we asked him to his face, he would only laugh, if he were drunk, and if he were sober, deny solemnly that he ever tasted anything but water.

He was not only useless as an officer, and a bad influence amongst the men, but it was plain that at this rate he must soon kill himself outright; so nobody was much surprised, nor very sorry, when one dark night, with a head sea, he disappeared entirely and was seen no more.

"Overboard!" said the captain. "Well, gentlemen, that saves the trouble of putting him in irons."

But there we were, without a mate; and it was necessary, of course, to advance one of the men. The boatswain, Job Anderson, was the likeliest man aboard, and, though he kept his old title, he served in a way as mate. Mr. Trelawney had followed the sea, and his knowledge made him very useful, for he often took a watch himself in easy weather. And the coxswain, Israel Hands, was a careful, wily, old, experienced seaman, who could be trusted at a pinch with almost anything.

He was a great confidant of Long John Silver, and so the mention of his name leads me on to speak of our ship's cook, Barbecue, as the men called him.

Aboard ship he carried his crutch by a lanyard round his neck, to have both hands as free as possible. It was something to see him wedge the foot of the crutch against a bulkhead, and propped against it, yielding to every movement of the ship, get on with his cooking, like some one safe ashore. Still more strange was it to see him in the heaviest of weather cross the deck. He had a line or two rigged up to help him across the widest spaces—Long John's earrings, they were called; and he would hand himself from one place to another, now using the crutch, now trailing it alongside by the lanyard, as quickly as another man could walk. Yet some of the men who had sailed with him before expressed their pity to see him so reduced.

"He's no common man, Barbecue," said the coxswain to me.

"He had good schooling in his young days, and can speak like a book when so minded; and brave—a lion's nothing alongside of Long John! I seen him grapple four, and knock their heads together—him unarmed."

All the crew respected and even obeyed him. He had a way of talking to each, and doing everybody some particular service. To me he was unweariedly kind; and always glad to see me in the galley, which he kept as clean as a new pin; the dishes hanging up burnished, and his parrot in a cage in one corner.

"Come away, Hawkins," he would say; "come and have a yarn with John. Nobody more welcome than yourself, my son. Sit you down and hear the news. Here's Cap'n Flint—I calls my parrot Cap'n Flint, after the famous buccaneer— here's Cap'n Flint predicting success to our v'yage. Wasn't you, cap'n?"

And the parrot would say, with great rapidity, "Pieces of eight! pieces of eight! pieces of eight!" till you wondered that it was not out of breath, or till John threw his handkerchief over the cage.

"Now, that bird," he would say, "is, maybe, two hundred years old, Hawkins—they lives for ever mostly; and if anybody's seen more wickedness, it must be the devil himself. She's sailed with England, the great Cap'n England, the pirate. She's been at Madagascar, and at Malabar, and Surinam, and Providence, and Portobello. She was at the fishing up of the wrecked plate ships. It's there she learned 'Pieces of eight,' and little wonder; three hundred and fifty thousand of 'em, Hawkins! She was at the boarding of the Viceroy of the Indies out of Goa, she was; and to look at her you would think she was a babby. But you smelt powder—didn't you, cap'n?"

"Stand by to go about," the parrot would scream.

"Ah, she's a handsome craft, she is," the cook would say, and give her sugar from his pocket, and then the bird would peck at the bars and swear straight on, passing belief for wickedness. "There," John would add, "you can't touch pitch and not be mucked, lad. Here's this poor old innocent bird o' mine swearing blue fire, and none the wiser, you may lay to that. She would swear the same, in a manner of speaking, before chaplain." And John would touch his forelock with a solemn way he had, that made me think he was the best of men.

In the meantime, the squire and Captain Smollett were still on pretty distant terms with one another. The squire made no bones about the matter; he despised the captain. The captain, on his part, never spoke but when he was spoken to, and then sharp and short and dry, and not a word wasted. He owned, when driven into a corner, that he seemed to have been wrong about the crew, that some of them were as brisk as he wanted to see, and all had behaved fairly well. As for the ship, he had taken a downright fancy to her. "She'll lie a point nearer the wind than a man has a right to expect of his own married wife, sir. But," he would add, "all I say is we're not home again, and I don't like the cruise."

The squire, at this, would turn away and march up and down the deck, chin in air.

"A trifle more of that man," he would say, "and I shall explode."

We had some heavy weather, which only proved the qualities of the *Hispaniola*. Every man on board seemed well content, and they must have been hard to please if they had been otherwise; for it is my belief there was never a ship's company so spoiled since Noah put to sea. Double grog was going on the least excuse; there was duff on odd days, as, for instance, if the squire heard it was any man's birthday; and always a barrel of apples standing broached in the waist, for any one to help himself that had a fancy.

"Never knew good come of it yet," the captain said to Dr. Livesey. "Spoil foc's'le hands, make devils. That's my belief."

But good did come of the apple barrel, as you shall hear; for if it had not been for that, we should have had no note of warning, and might all have perished by the hand of treachery.

This was how it came about.

We had run up the trades to get the wind of the island we were after—I am not allowed to be more plain—and now we were running down for it with a bright look-out day and night. It was about the last day of our outward voyage, by the largest computation; some time that night, or, at latest, before noon of the morrow, we should sight the Treasure Island. We were heading SSW, and had a steady breeze abeam and a quiet sea. The *Hispaniola* rolled steadily, dipping her bowsprit now and then with a whiff of spray. All was drawing alow and aloft; every one was in the bravest spirits, because we were now so near an end of the first part of our adventure.

Now, just after sundown, when all my work was over, and I was on my way to my berth, it occurred to me that I should like an apple. I ran on deck. The watch was all forward looking out for the island. The man at the helm was watching the luff of the sail, and whistling away gently to himself; and that was the only sound excepting the swish of the sea against the bows and around the sides of the ship.

In I got bodily into the apple barrel, and found there was scarce an apple left; but, sitting down there in the dark, what with the sound of the waters and the rocking movement of the ship, I had either fallen asleep, or was on the point of doing so, when a heavy man sat down with rather a clash close by. The barrel shook as he leaned his shoulders against it, and I was just about to jump up when the man began to speak. It was Silver's voice, and, before I had heard a dozen words, I would not have shown myself for all the world, but lay there, trembling and listening, in the extreme of fear and curiosity; for from these dozen words I understood that the lives of all the honest men aboard depended upon me alone.

"No, not I," said Silver. "Flint was cap'n; I was quartermaster, along of my timber leg. The same broadside I lost my leg, old Pew lost his dead-lights. It was a master surgeon, him that ampytated me—out of college and all—Latin by the bucket, and what not; but he was hanged like a dog, and sun-dried, like the rest, at Corso Castle. That was Roberts' men, that was, and comed of changing names to their ships—*Royal Fortune* and so on. Now, what a ship was christened, so let her stay, I says. So it was with the *Cassandra,* as brought us all safe home from Malabar, after England took the Viceroy of the Indies; so it was with the old *Walrus,* Flint's old ship, as I've seen a-muck with the red blood and fit to sink with gold."

"Ah!" cried another voice, that of the youngest hand on board, and evidently full of admiration, "he was the flower of the flock, was Flint!"

"Davis was a man, too, by all accounts," said Silver. "I never sailed along of him; first with England, then with Flint, that's my story; and now here on my account, in a manner of speaking. I laid by nine hundred safe, from England, and two thousand after Flint. That ain't bad for a man before the mast—all safe in bank. 'Tain't earning now, it's saving does it, you may lay to that. Where's all England's men now? I dunno. Where's Flint's? Why, most on 'em aboard here, and glad to get the duff—been begging before that, some on 'em. Old Pew, as had lost his sight, and might have thought shame, spends twelve hundred pound in a year, like a lord in Parliament. Where is he now? Well, he's dead now and under hatches; but for two year before that, shiver my timbers! the man was starving. He begged, and he stole, and he cut throats, and starved at that by the powers!"

"Well, it ain't much use, after all," said the young seaman.

" 'Tain't much use for fools, you may lay to it—that, nor nothing," cried Silver. "But now, you look here: you're young, you are, but you're as smart as paint. I see that when I set my eyes on you, and I'll talk to you like a man."

You may imagine how I felt when I heard this abominable old rogue addressing another in the very same words of flattery as he had used to myself. I think, if I had been able, that I would have killed him through the barrel. Meantime, he ran on, little supposing he was overheard.

"Here it is about gentlemen of fortune. They lives rough, and they risk swinging, but they eat and drink like fighting-cocks, and when a cruise is done, why, it's hundreds of pounds instead of hundreds of farthings in their pockets. Now, the most goes for rum and a good fling, and to sea again in their shirts. But that's not the course I lay. I puts it all away, some here, some there, and none too much anywheres, by reason of suspicion. I'm fifty, mark you; once back from this cruise, I set up gentleman in earnest. Time enough, too, says you. Ah, but I've lived easy in the meantime; never denied myself o' nothing heart desires, and slep' soft and ate dainty all my days, but when at sea. And how did I begin? Before the mast, like you!"

"Well," said the other, "but all the other money's gone now, ain't it? You daren't show face in Bristol after this."

"Why, where might you suppose it was?" asked Silver, derisively.

"At Bristol, in banks and places," answered his companion.

"It were," said the cook; "it were when we weighed anchor. But my old missis has it all by now. And the 'Spy-glass' is sold, lease and goodwill and rigging; and the old girl's off to meet me. I would tell you where, for I trust you; but it 'u'd make jealousy among the mates."

"And can you trust your missis?" asked the other.

"Gentlemen of fortune," returned the cook, "usually trusts little among themselves, and right they are, you may lay to it. But I have a way with me, I have. When a mate brings a slip on his cable—one as knows me, I mean—it won't be in the same world with old John. There was some that was feared of Pew, and some that was feared of Flint; but Flint his own self was feared of me. Feared he was, and proud. They was the roughest crew afloat, was Flint's; the devil himself would have been feared to go to sea with them. Well, now, I tell you, I'm not a boasting man, and you seen yourself how easy I keep company; but when I was quartermaster, *lambs* wasn't the word for Flint's old buccaneers. Ah, you may be sure of yourself in old John's ship."

"Well, I tell you now," replied the lad, "I didn't half a quarter like the job till I had this talk with you, John; but there's my hand on it now."

"And a brave lad you were, and smart, too," answered Silver, shaking hands so heartily that all the barrel shook, "and a finer figurehead for a gentleman of fortune I never clapped my eyes on."

By this time I had begun to understand the meaning of their terms. By a "gentleman of fortune" they plainly meant neither more nor less than a common pirate, and the little scene that I had overheard was the last act in the corruption of one of the honest hands—perhaps of the last one left aboard. But on this point I was soon to be relieved, for, Silver giving a little whistle, a third man strolled up and sat down by the party.

"Dick's square," said Silver.

"Oh, I know'd Dick was square," returned the voice of the coxswain, Israel Hands. "He's no fool is Dick." And he turned his quid and spat. "But, look here," he went on, "here's what I want to know, Barbecue: how long are we a-going to stand off and on like a blessed bumboat? I've had a'most enough o' Cap'n

Smollett; he's hazed me long enough, by thunder! I want to go into that cabin, I do. I want their pickles and wines, and that."

"Israel," said Silver, "your head ain't much account, nor ever was. But you're able to hear, I reckon; leastways, your ears is big enough. Now, here's what I say: you'll berth forward, and you'll live hard, and you'll speak soft, and you'll keep sober, till I give the word; and you may lay to that, my son."

"Well, I don't say no, do I?" growled the coxswain. "What I say is, when? That's what I say."

"When! by the powers!" cried Silver. "Well, now, if you want to know, I'll tell you when. The last moment I can manage; and that's when. Here's a first-rate seaman, Cap'n Smollett, sails the blessed ship for us. Here's the squire and doctor with a map and such—I don't know where it is, do I? No more do you, says you. Well, then, I mean this squire and doctor shall find the stuff, and help us to get it aboard, by the powers! Then we'll see. If I was sure of you all, sons of double Dutchmen, I'd have Cap'n Smollett navigate us half-way back again before I struck."

"Why, we're all seamen aboard here, I should think," said the lad Dick.

"We're all foc's'le hands, you mean," snapped Silver. "We can steer a course, but who's to set one? That's what all you gentlemen split on, first and last. If I had my way, I'd have Cap'n Smollett work us back into the trades at least: then we'd have no blessed miscalculations and a spoonful of water a day. But I know the sort you are. I'll finish with 'em at the island, as soon's the blunt's on board, and a pity it is. But you're never happy till you're drunk. Split my sides, I've a sick heart to sail with the likes of you!"

"Easy all, Long John," cried Israel. "Who's a-crossin' of you?"

"Why, how many tall ships, think ye, now, have I seen laid aboard? And how many brisk lads drying in the sun at Execution Dock?" cried Silver, "and all for this same hurry and hurry and hurry. You hear me? I seen a thing or two at sea, I have. If you would on'y lay your course, and a p'int to windward, you would ride in carriages, you would. But not you! I know you. You'll have your mouthful of rum to-morrow, and go hang."

"Everybody know'd you was a kind of a chapling, John; but

there's others as could hand and steer as well as you," said Israel. "They liked a bit o' fun, they did. They wasn't so high and dry, nohow, but took their fling, like jolly companions every one."

"So?" says Silver. "Well, and where are they now? Pew was that sort, and he died a beggar-man. Flint was, and he died of rum at Savannah. Ah, they was a sweet crew, they was! on'y, where are they?"

"But," asked Dick, "when we do lay 'em athwart, what are we to do with 'em, anyhow?"

"There's the man for me!" cried the cook, admiringly. "That's what I call business. Well, what would you think? Put 'em ashore like maroons? That would have been England's way. Or cut 'em down like that much pork? That would have been Flint's or Billy Bones's."

"Billy was the man for that," said Israel. " 'Dead men don't bite,' says he. Well, he's dead now hisself; he knows the long and short on it now; and if ever a rough hand come to port, it was Billy."

"Right you are," said Silver, "rough and ready. But mark you here: I'm an easy man—I'm quite the gentleman, says you; but this time it's serious. Dooty is dooty, mates. I give my vote—death. When I'm in Parlyment, and riding in my coach, I don't want none of these sea-lawyers in the cabin a-coming home, unlooked for, like the devil at prayers. Wait is what I say; but when the time comes, why let her rip!"

"John," cries the coxswain, "you're a man!"

"You'll say so, Israel, when you see," said Silver. "Only one thing I claim—I claim Trelawney. I'll wring his calf's head off his body with these hands. Dick!" he added, breaking off, "you just jump up like a sweet lad, and get me an apple, to wet my pipe like."

You may fancy the terror I was in! I should have leaped out and run for it, if I had found the strength; but my limbs and heart alike misgave me. I heard Dick begin to rise, and then some one seemingly stopped him, and the voice of Hands exclaimed:

"Oh, stow that! Don't you get sucking of that bilge, John. Let's have a go of the rum."

"Dick," said Silver, "I trust you. I've a gauge on the keg, mind. There's the key; you fill a pannikin and bring it up."

Terrified as I was, I could not help thinking to myself that this must have been how Mr. Arrow got the strong waters that destroyed him.

Dick was gone but a little while, and during his absence Israel spoke straight on in the cook's ear. It was but a word or two that I could catch, and yet I gathered some important news; for, besides other scraps that tended to the same purpose, this whole clause was audible: "Not another man of them'll jine." Hence there were still faithful men on board.

When Dick returned, one after another of the trio took the pannikin and drank—one "To luck"; another with a "Here's to old Flint"; and Silver himself saying, in a kind of song, "Here's to ourselves, and hold your luff, plenty of prizes and plenty of duff."

Just then a sort of brightness fell upon me in the barrel, and, looking up, I found the moon had risen, and was silvering the mizzen-top and shining white on the luff of the fore-sail; and almost at the same time the voice of the look-out shouted, "Land ho!"

There was a great rush of feet across the deck. I could hear people tumbling up from the cabin and the foc's'le; and, slipping in an instant outside my barrel, I dived behind the fore-sail, made a double towards the stern, and came out upon the open deck in time to join Hunter and Dr. Livesey in the rush for the weather bow.

There all hands were already congregated. A belt of fog had lifted almost simultaneously with the appearance of the moon. Away to the southwest of us we saw two low hills, about a couple of miles apart, and rising behind one of them a third and higher hill, whose peak was still buried in the fog. All three seemed sharp and conical in figure.

So much I saw, almost in a dream, for I had not yet recovered from my horrid fear of a minute or two before. And then I heard the voice of Captain Smollett issuing orders. The *Hispaniola* was laid a couple of points nearer the wind, and now sailed a course that would just clear the island on the east.

"And now, men," said the captain, when all was sheeted home, "has any one of you ever seen that land ahead?"

"I have, sir," said Silver. "I've watered there with a trader I was cook in."

"The anchorage is on the south, behind an islet, I fancy?" asked the captain.

"Yes, sir; Skeleton Island they calls it. It were a main place for pirates once, and a hand we had on board knowed all their names for it. That hill to the nor'ard they calls the Fore-mast Hill; there are three hills in a row running south'ard—fore, main, and mizzen, sir. But the main—that's the big 'un, with the cloud on it—they usually calls the Spy-glass, by reason of a look-out they kept when they was in the anchorage cleaning; for it's there they cleaned their ships, sir, asking your pardon."

"I have a chart here," says Captain Smollett. "See if that's the place."

Long John's eyes burned in his head as he took the chart; but, by the fresh look of the paper, I knew he was doomed to disappointment. This was not the map we found in Billy Bones's chest, but an accurate copy, complete in all things—names and heights and soundings—with the single exception of the red crosses and the written notes. Sharp as must have been his annoyance, Silver had the strength of mind to hide it.

"Yes, sir," said he, "this is the spot, to be sure; and very prettily drawed out. Who might have done that, I wonder? The pirates were too ignorant, I reckon. Ay, here it is: 'Capt. Kidd's Anchorage'—just the name my shipmate called it. There's a strong current runs along the south, and then away nor'ard up the west coast. Right you was, sir," says he, "to haul your wind and keep the weather of the island. Leastways, if such was your intention as to enter and careen, and there ain't no better place for that in these waters."

"Thank you, my man," says Captain Smollett. "I'll ask you, later on, to give us a help. You may go."

I was surprised at the coolness with which John avowed his knowledge of the island; and I own I was half frightened when I saw him drawing near to myself. He did not know, to be sure, that I had overheard his council from the apple barrel, and yet I had, by this time, taken such a horror of his cruelty, duplicity, and power, that I could scarce conceal a shudder when he laid his hand upon my arm.

"Ah," says he, "this here is a sweet spot, this island—a sweet spot for a lad to get ashore on. You'll bathe, and you'll climb trees, and you'll hunt goats, you will; and you'll get aloft on them hills like a goat yourself. Why, it makes me young again. I was going to forget my timber leg, I was. It's a pleasant thing to be young, and have ten toes, and you may lay to that. When you want to go a bit of exploring, you just ask old John, and he'll put up a snack for you to take along."

And clapping me in the friendliest way upon the shoulder, he hobbled off forward, and went below.

Captain Smollett, the squire, and Dr. Livesey were talking together on the quarter-deck, and, anxious as I was to tell them my story, I durst not interrupt them openly. While I was still casting about in my thoughts to find some probable excuse, Dr. Livesey called me to his side. He had left his pipe below, and being a slave to tobacco, had meant that I should fetch it; but as soon as I was near enough to speak and not to be overheard, I broke out immediately: "Doctor, let me speak. Get the captain and squire down to the cabin, and then make some pretence to send for me. I have terrible news."

The doctor changed countenance a little, but next moment he was master of himself.

"Thank you, Jim," said he, quite loudly, "that was all I wanted to know," as if he had asked me a question.

And with that he turned on his heel and rejoined the other two. They spoke together for a little, and though none of them started, or raised his voice, or so much as whistled, it was plain enough that Dr. Livesey had communicated my request; for the next thing that I heard was the captain giving an order to Job Anderson, and all hands were piped on deck.

"My lads," said Captain Smollett, "I've a word to say to you. This land that we have sighted is the place we have been sailing for. Mr. Trelawney, being a very open-handed gentleman, as we all know, has just asked me a word or two, and as I was able to tell him that every man on board had done his duty, alow and aloft, as I never ask to see it done better, why, he and I and the doctor are going below to the cabin to drink *your* health and luck, and you'll have grog served out for you to drink *our* health and luck. I'll tell you what I think of this: I think it handsome. And if you think as I do, you'll give a good sea cheer for the gentleman that does it."

The cheer followed—that was a matter of course, but it rang out so full and hearty, that I confess I could hardly believe these same men were plotting for our blood.

"One more cheer for Cap'n Smollett," cried Long John, when the first had subsided.

And this also was given with a will.

On the top of that the three gentlemen went below, and not long after, word was sent forward that Jim Hawkins was wanted in the cabin.

I found them all three seated round the table, a bottle of Spanish wine and some raisins before them, and the doctor smoking away, with his wig on his lap, and that, I knew, was a sign that he was agitated. The stern window was open, for it was a warm night, and you could see the moon shining behind on the ship's wake.

"Now, Hawkins," said the squire, "you have something to say. Speak up."

I did as I was bid, and as short as I could make it, told the whole details of Silver's conversation. Nobody interrupted me till I was done, nor did any one of the three of them make so much as a movement, but they kept their eyes upon my face from first to last.

"Jim," said Dr. Livesey, "take a seat."

And they made me sit down at table beside them, poured me out a glass of wine, filled my hands with raisins, and all three, one after the other, and each with a bow, drank my good health, and their service to me, for my luck and courage.

"Now, captain," said the squire, "you were right and I was wrong. I own myself an ass, and I await your orders."

"No more an ass than I, sir," returned the captain. "I never heard of a crew that meant to mutiny but what showed signs before, for any man that had an eye in his head to see the mischief and take steps according. But this crew," he added, "beats me."

"Captain," said the doctor, "with your permission, that's Silver. A very remarkable man."

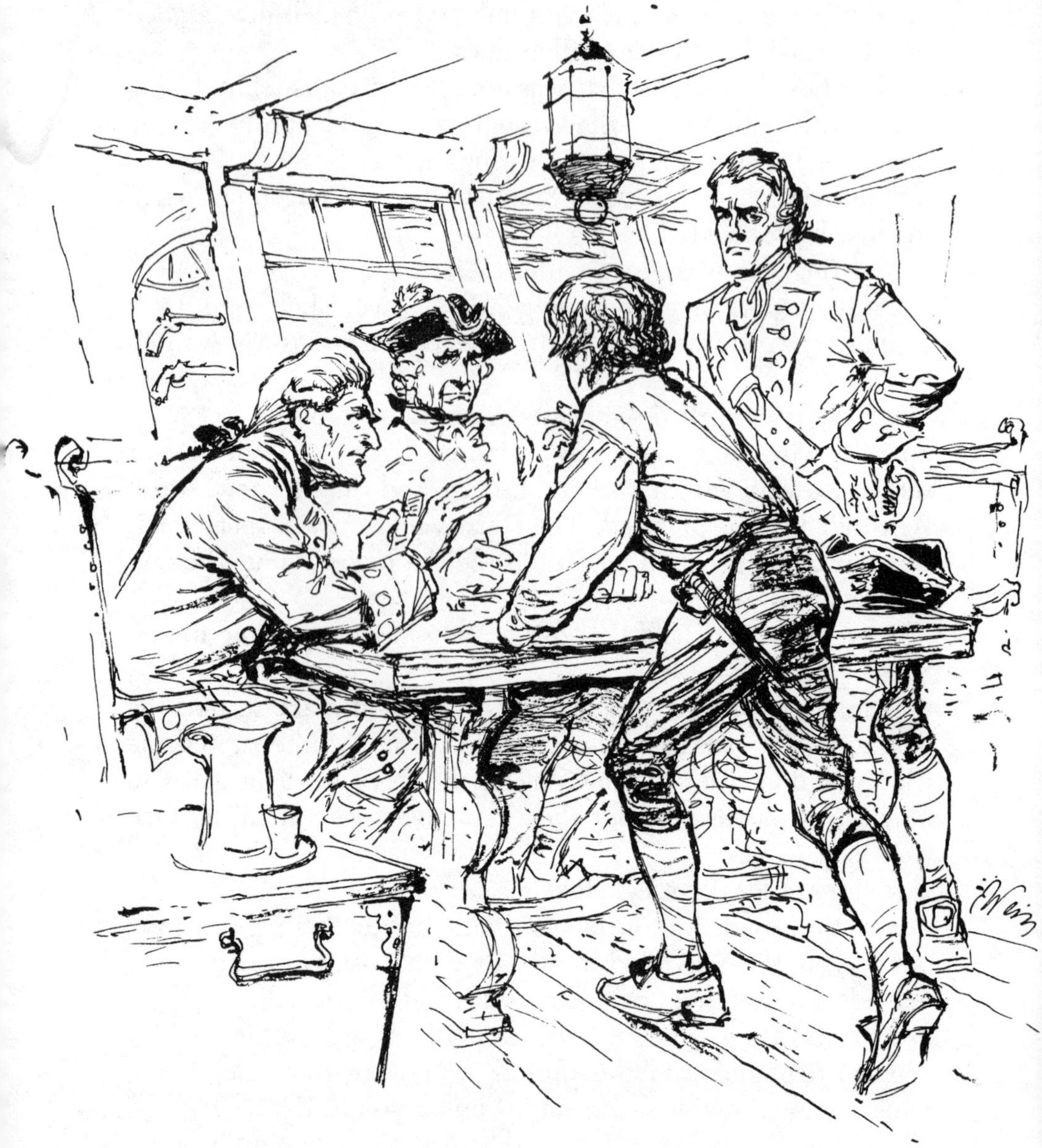

"He'd look remarkably well from a yard-arm, sir," returned the captain. "But this is talk; this don't lead to anything. I see three or four points, and with Mr. Trelawney's permission, I'll name them."

"You, sir, are the captain. It is for you to speak," says Mr. Trelawney, grandly.

"First point," began Mr. Smollett. "We must go on, because we can't turn back. If I gave the word to go about, they would rise at once. Second point, we have time before us—at least, until this treasure's found. Third point, there are faithful hands. Now, sir, it's got to come to blows sooner or later; and what I propose is, to take time by the forelock, as the saying is, and come to blows some fine day when they least expect it. We can count, I take it, on your own home servants, Mr. Trelawney?"

"As upon myself," declared the squire.

"Three," reckoned the captain, "ourselves make seven, counting Hawkins, here. Now, about the honest hands."

"Most likely Trelawney's own men," said the doctor; "those he had picked up for himself, before he lit on Silver."

"Nay," replied the squire, "Hands was one of mine."

"I did think I could have trusted Hands," added the captain.

"And to think that they're all Englishmen!" broke out the squire. "Sir, I could find it in my heart to blow the ship up."

"Well, gentlemen," said the captain, "the best that I can say is not much. We must lay to, if you please, and keep a bright lookout. It's trying on a man, I know. It would be pleasanter to come to blows. But there's no help for it till we know our men. Lay to, and whistle for a wind, that's my view."

"Jim here," said the doctor, "can help us more than any one. The men are not shy with him, and Jim is a noticing lad."

"Hawkins, I put prodigious faith in you," added the squire.

I began to feel pretty desperate at this, for I felt altogether helpless; and yet, by an odd train of circumstances, it was indeed through me that safety came.

Treasure Island, *first published in 1882, is but one of Robert Louis Stevenson's great novels, among which are such works as* Kidnapped *and* The Strange Case of Dr. Jekyll and Mr. Hyde.

Call It Courage

BY ARMSTRONG SPERRY

Illustrations by the author

Rather than cringe in the face of his terrible fear of the sea, Mafatu, son of a Polynesian chief, decides to conquer his weakness. With only his dog Uri for companionship, the boy sets out in a small boat. For a while, Kivi the albatross seems to guide the little craft.

DAY broke over a gray and dismal world. The canoe lifted and fell idly on the glassy swells. Mafatu looked back over his shoulder, searching the horizon for a last glimpse of Hikueru; but the atoll had vanished, as if to hide itself forever from his concern.

The matting sail slatted uselessly. But there seemed to be no need of a sail: the little canoe was riding one of the mysterious ocean currents that flow in their courses through the length and breadth of the Pacific: the *Ara Moana,* Paths of the Sea, as the Ancients called them. They were the ocean currents that had carried the Polynesian navigators from island to island in the childhood of the world. Mafatu was drifting farther and farther away from his homeland.

With wide-flapping wings Kivi rose from the bow of the canoe. In ascending spirals the bird climbed higher and higher, until at last he was no more than a gray speck against the lighter gray of the sky. Mafatu watched his albatross disappear and felt a desolation flood his heart. Now there was only Uri to keep him company in this hostile world of sky and sea. Uri. . . . The yellow dog lay curled up in the shadow of the bow, opening one eye from time to time to look at his master. Wherever Mafatu went, Uri, too, would go.

All around, as far as the eye could reach, were wastes of leaden water. The canoe was the moving center of a limitless circle of sea. The boy shuddered. His fingers gripped the paddle convulsively. He thought of Kana and the other boys—what would they say when they learned that he had disappeared? And Tavana Nui—would there be sorrow in his father's heart? Would he believe that Moana, the Sea God, had claimed his son at last?

It was an ominous, oppressive world at this season of storm. Half a mile distant a whale heaved its varnished hulk to the surface, to throw a jet of vapory mist high into the air; then it submerged, leaving scarcely a ripple to mark its passage. A shoal of flying fishes broke water, skimming away in a silver shimmer of flight. A dolphin sped after them, smooth-rolling in pursuit, so close that the boy could hear the sound of its breathing. This world of the sea was ruled by Nature's harsh law of survival. Mafatu knew the sea with an intimacy given to few. He had seen fleets of giant mantas whipping the lagoon of Hikueru to a boiling fury; he had seen the mighty cachalot set upon by killer-whales and torn to ribbons almost in the blink of an eye; once he had seen an octopus as large as the trunk of a tamanu, with tentacles thirty feet long, rise from the mile-deep water beyond the barrier-reef. . . . *Ai*, this sea!

Mafatu opened one of the green drinking nuts and tilted back his head to let the cool liquid trickle down his parched throat; more refreshing than spring water, cool on the hottest days, and as sustaining as food. The boy scooped out the gelatinous meat for Uri and the dog ate it gratefully.

The ocean current which held the canoe in its grip seemed to have quickened. There was a wind rising, too, in little puffs and gusts. Now the canoe heeled over under the sudden attack, while Mafatu scrambled onto the outrigger to lend his weight for ballast; then the wind dropped as suddenly as it appeared, while the canoe righted itself and the boy breathed freely once again. He searched the skies for Kivi. His albatross might have been one of a thousand sea birds flying against the roof of the sky, or he might have vanished utterly, leaving his friends here in solitary space. The bird had led Mafatu out through the reef-passage at Hikueru into the open ocean, and now, it seemed, had deserted him.

A storm was making, moving in out of those mysterious belts which lie north and south of the equator, the home of hurricanes. The wind shifted a point, bringing with it a heavy squall. Mafatu lowered the sail on the run and gripped the steering paddle with hands that showed white at the knuckles. All

around him now was a world of tumbling water, gray in the hollows, greenish on the slopes. The wind tore off the combing crests and flung the spray at the sky. Like advance scouts of an oncoming army, wind gusts moved down upon the canoe, struck at it savagely. So busy was Mafatu with the paddle that there was no time for thought. He called a prayer to Maui, God of the Fishermen:

"Maui é! E matai tu!"

Somehow the sound of his own voice reassured him. Uri lifted his head, cocked his ears, thumped his tail for a second. The canoe rose to the swells as lightly as a gull and coasted like a sled down the frothing slopes. What skill had wrought this small canoe! This dugout, hewn from the mighty tamanu tree. It swooped and yielded, bucked and scudded, one with the fierce element whose back it rode.

The sky darkened. A burst of lightning lit up the sea with supernatural brilliance. An instantaneous crack of thunder shattered the world. Lightning again, striking at the hissing water. Mafatu watched it with fascinated eyes. Now it was all about him. It ran to the end of the boom in globes of fire that exploded and vanished, and in the awful moment of its being it revealed mountain shapes of dark water, heaving, shouldering.

. . . How long could this frail craft of wood and sennit resist? Under the combined attack of wind and sea it seemed that something must inevitably give way. The wind shrilled a fiercer note. Spray stung the boy's flesh, blinded his eyes, chilled his marrow.

The sail went first—with a split and a roar. Fragments swept off on the back of the wind. The cords that held the mast hummed like plucked wires. Then with a rending groan the mast cracked. Before Mafatu could leap to cut it clear, it snapped off and disappeared in a churn of black water. The boy clung to the paddle, fighting to keep his canoe from turning broadside. Water swept aboard and out again. Only the buoyancy of tamanu kept the craft afloat. Uri cowered in the bow, half submerged, his howls drowned by the roar of the elements. Mafatu gripped his paddle for very life, an unreasoning terror powering his arms. This sea that he had always feared was rising to claim him, just as it had claimed his mother. How rightly he had feared it! Moana, the Sea God, had been biding his time. . . . "Someday, Mafatu, I will claim you!"

The boy lost all sense of time's passage. Every nerve became dulled by tumult. The wind howled above his head and still Mafatu clung to the lashed steering paddle; clung fast long after strength had vanished and only the will to live locked his strong fingers about the shaft. Even death would not loose the grip of those fingers. He held his little craft true to the wind.

There was a wave lifting before the canoe. Many the boy had seen, but this was a giant—a monster livid and hungry. Higher, higher it rose, until it seemed that it must scrape at the low-hanging clouds. Its crest heaved over with a vast sigh. The boy saw it coming. He tried to cry out. No sound issued from his throat. Suddenly the wave was upon him. Down it crashed. *Chaos!* Mafatu felt the paddle torn from his hands. Thunder in his ears. Water strangling him. Terror in his soul. The canoe slewed round into the trough. The boy flung himself forward, wound his arms about the mid-thwart. It was the end of a world.

The wave passed. Stunned, gasping, Mafatu raised his head and looked about. For a second he could not believe that he still breathed and had being. He saw Uri wedged under the bow, choking for air. He pulled the dog free. Then he saw that his string of drinking nuts had vanished. His fish spear was gone. The knife that hung about his neck by a twist of bark had been torn away. Even his *pareu* of fiber tapa fell from his body as water soaked it through. He was naked, defenseless, without food or weapon, hurled forward on the breath of the hurricane. Numb of all feeling, empty as a shell, still he clung to life, and the hours droned by. . . .

So gradual was the storm's easing that at first the boy was

unaware of it. The wind was blowing itself out, moving off into the empty spaces of the world. Uri crept toward the prostrate boy, quailing beside him, whimpering softly.

Night came and passed.

There was no morning mist to dim the splendor of the sunburst across the swinging seas. Far away the wings of an albatross caught its gold as it wheeled and planed against the roof of heaven. The only hint of recent storm lay in the rough and tumbling waters. As the sun climbed through the hot hours of morning, it burned into the boy's body like the sacred fires of the great marae of Hikueru. Mafatu's skin blistered and cracked. His tongue swelled in his throat. He tried to call out a prayer to Maui, but his voice was thick; the sounds which came forth were no more than a hoarse cry. The canoe, stripped of sail and mast, without a paddle to guide it in the swift-racing current, twisted and shifted in the rushing waters.

As one hour merged into another there came moments of fitful, choking slumber, a growing agony of thirst for the boy and his dog. The sun burned into them like an inescapable eye. The current which held Mafatu's canoe fast in its grip was bearing it swiftly on toward its mysterious destination.

And thus the day passed, while night once more descended, bringing blessed release from the sun.

Now the air was luminous with promise of another day. Out of the sultry mists the sea emerged, blue and violent. With the coming of this new day terror raised its head. Mafatu tried to fight it back, to deny its existence; but it gripped his heart with clammy fingers, tightened his throat. He flung himself flat on the floor of the canoe and buried his face in his arms. He must have cried out then. His voice was but a hoarse croak, yet it stirred Uri to life: the dog's ragged tail gave one feeble thump. With the ghost of a whimper the animal laid his hot nose against the boy's hand.

The brave thump of his dog's tail touched Mafatu profoundly. He caught the animal to him, while a new assurance, a new strength, flooded his being. If Uri could have courage to die, surely he, Mafatu, could not do less! In that instant he heard a whir and fury in the sky above, a beat of wide wings. . . . Looking upward, the boy's dulled eyes made out the widespread wings of an albatross, circling above the canoe.

"Kivi!" Mafatu cried hoarsely. "*Ai,* Kivi!"

Even as he spoke, the bird wheeled slowly, then flew off straight ahead for the distant horizon. The boy noticed then that the sea current was carrying him almost due southwest. Kivi's flight moved in exact parallel. Once more it seemed as if his albatross were leading him onward, just as he had led the canoe out of the passage of Hikueru.

Mafatu scanned the rim of the horizon; it looked as hard as the cut edge of a stone. But suddenly the boy's heart gave a great leap and he started forward. *It couldn't be!* It was a cloud. . . . But the sky was cloudless. Far off in the sea-shimmer lay something that was neither sea nor sky. The swells, lifting higher, now revealed, now concealed it. That shadow on the horizon —it was land! The boy flung himself forward, shaking uncontrollably.

He seized Uri in his arms and lifted him up, laughing, crying: "Uri! Uri! It's land. *Land!*"

The dog sniffed at the air and a little whimper broke from him.

What island could this be? Was it Tahiti, the golden island, whose language was akin to that of Hikueru? Or was it, perhaps, one of the terrible dark islands of the eaters-of-men?

Now the current had a westward drift, and it was to the west that the dark islands lay. . . .

All day, as the canoe drifted onward, the boy watched the distant shadow-shape of land, not daring to take his eyes from it lest it vanish into the sea. Hunger and thirst were lulled into forgetfulness. There was only this one reality, land—escape from the sea. Weak as he was, he still clung to the thwart, his lips whispering a silent prayer of gratitude. With waning afternoon, the island took more distinct form as the canoe drifted nearer. It was high and peaked, its valleys blue-shadowed against the paler tone of the sky. Hour by hour, with every lift of the swells, the island rose higher and higher, filling Mafatu's soul with wonder. Hikueru, the only land he had ever seen, was as flat as his hand; but a great single peak crowned this strange island. Trees rose green and fair, tier upon tier of them, from the shoreline into the foothills of the purple mountain. Uri had caught the scent of the land now and was quivering with delight.

Then from far off came the first muffled thunder of the reef: the boom of the surf high-bursting on the barrier coral. That sound—was it the voice of Moana? "Someday, Mafatu, someday." . . . Involuntarily the boy shuddered. Would his ears never be free of the Sea God's threat?

Mafatu was powerless to guide his craft. He sensed that the current had quickened. He could only watch helplessly as the little canoe, swift as the following gulls, rushed to meet the tides of the island where they met and churned in a cross sea of conflict. Now across the swells came a sound like a chorus of ghostly fishermen weary with their day's toil: sea birds, always complaining, never at rest; while softer, yet rising above it was another sound—the voice of the reef itself, quieting with sundown, like the reassuring hush of a mother to her child.

Night stole up from the face of the sea, enveloping the world. There was no moon, but the black sky was spangled with unguessed millions of stars: other worlds, other suns. To the watching boy, with land in the offing, they seemed closer and more friendly. The bottom star of the Southern Cross pointed to the end of the world. . . . A soft land breeze, heavy with a scent of flowers, wafted out across the dark waters, tantalizing, bitter-sweet.

Weak with thirst, the boy drifted now into a merciful sleep. He struggled against it, like a weary swimmer fighting a riptide, but his head drooped and his eyes closed.

He was aroused at midnight by a thunderous tumult in his ears. Of a sudden he felt the canoe under him lifted and flung high into the air. Then down it crashed into splinters upon the reef. Boy and dog were hurled headlong into the boiling surf.

The shock of cold water brought Mafatu half back to consciousness. Blindly he struck out, fighting for survival. Uri—where was he? No sign of the dog. The boy was aware that the canoe must have been flung over the barrier-reef, for here the water was scarcely troubled by wind or tide. Now he was

swimming, swimming. . . . Somewhere ahead a strip of beach, salt-white in the darkness, lured him onward. His muscles did it of themselves. Only a will to live. A strip of sand white in the night. . . . He caught the gleam of a shark's belly, close at hand, but on he swam. His unhampered limbs moved freely through the water.

Of a sudden there was something solid beneath his feet. Sand. Mafatu stumbled, staggered, fell to his knees in the shallows. His lips moved in dry, soundless speech. Lying there with the water rippling and breaking over him, he pulled himself half upright, swayed onward. The palms, trooping to the edge of the beach, were motionless in the night air. All the world seemed to hold its breath as this boy climbed up out of the sea.

He fell to the sand once more, then, guided by he knew not what impulse, he dragged himself to the edge of the jungle. A murmur of water reached his ears, soft as a chuckle of pleasant laughter. Water, sweet water. . . . Down the face of an age-worn rock a small cascade lost itself amid ferns and cool mosses. A ragged, strangling cry broke from Mafatu's throat. He stood upright to full height. Then he crashed to the mossy bank. One cheek lay in the cool water.

The moon lifted above the rim of the palms. It outlined in silver the form of a boy thin with hunger, naked as the daystar. It revealed a small wet dog, dragging himself across the beach to his master's side.

Mafatu lay without moving. Before Uri drank, he touched the boy's cheek with his hot muzzle.

Call It Courage ***was awarded the Newbery Medal in 1941.***

The Gold Bug

BY EDGAR ALLAN POE

Illustrations by Warren Chappell

Edgar Allan Poe, generally recognized as one of the world's great short-story writers, has few equals anywhere in the realm of the mystery and horror tale. Perhaps his most famous story is* The Gold Bug*, given here in its entirety.

> What ho! what ho! this fellow is dancing mad!
> He hath been bitten by the Tarantula.
> —*"All in the Wrong"*

MANY years ago, I contracted an intimacy with a Mr. William Legrand. He was of an ancient Huguènot family, and had once been wealthy; but a series of misfortunes had reduced him to want. To avoid the mortification consequent upon his disasters, he left New Orleans, the city of his forefathers, and took up his residence at Sullivan's Island, near Charleston, South Carolina.

This island is a very singular one. It consists of little else than the sea sand, and is about three miles long. Its breadth at no point exceeds a quarter of a mile. It is separated from the mainland by a scarcely perceptible creek, oozing its way through a wilderness of reeds and slime, a favorite resort of the marsh-hen. The vegetation, as might be supposed, is scant, or at least dwarfish. No trees of any magnitude are to be seen. Near the western extremity, where Fort Moultrie stands, and where are some miserable frame buildings, tenanted, during summer, by the fugitives from Charleston dust and fever, may be found, indeed, the bristly palmetto; but the whole island, with the exception of this western point, and a line of hard, white beach on the seacoast, is covered with a dense undergrowth of the sweet myrtle, so much prized by the horticulturists of England. The shrub here often attains the height of fifteen or twenty feet, and forms an almost impenetrable copice, burthening the air with its fragrance.

In the inmost recesses of this copice, not far from the eastern or more remote end of the island, Legrand had built himself a small hut, which he occupied when I first, by mere accident, made his acquaintance. This soon ripened into friendship—for there was much in the recluse to excite interest and esteem. I found him well educated, with unusual powers of mind, but infected with misanthropy, and subject to perverse moods of alternate enthusiasm and melancholy. He had with him many books, but rarely employed them. His chief amusements were gunning and fishing, or sauntering along the beach and through the myrtles, in quest of shells or entomological specimens—his collection of the latter might have been envied by a Swammer-damm. In these excursions he was usually accompanied by an old negro, called Jupiter, who had been manumitted before the reverses of the family, but who could be induced, neither by threats nor by promises, to abandon what he considered his right of attendance upon the footsteps of his young "Massa Will." It is not improbable that the relatives of Legrand, conceiving him to be somewhat unsettled in intellect, had contrived to instil this obstinacy into Jupiter, with a view to the supervision and guardianship of the wanderer.

The winters in the latitude of Sullivan's Island are seldom very severe, and in the fall of the year it is a rare event indeed when a fire is considered necessary. About the middle of October, 18—, there occurred, however, a day of remarkable chilliness. Just before sunset I scrambled my way through the evergreens to the hut of my friend, whom I had not visited for several weeks—my residence being, at that time, in Charleston, a distance of nine miles from the Island, while the facilities of passage and re-passage were very far behind those of the present day. Upon reaching the hut I rapped, as was my custom, and getting no reply, sought for the key where I knew it was secreted, unlocked the door and went in. A fine fire was blazing upon the hearth. It was a novelty, and by no means an ungrateful one. I threw off an overcoat, took an arm chair by the crackling logs, and awaited patiently the arrival of my hosts.

Soon after dark they arrived, and gave me a most cordial welcome. Jupiter, grinning from ear to ear, bustled about to prepare some marsh-hens for supper. Legrand was in one of his fits—how else shall I term them?—of enthusiasm. He had found an unknown bivalve, forming a new genus, and, more than this, he had hunted down and secured, with Jupiter's assistance, a *scarabaeus* which he believed to be totally new, but in respect to which he wished to have my opinion on the morrow.

"And why not tonight?" I asked, rubbing my hands over the blaze, and wishing the whole tribe of *scarabaei* at the devil.

"Ah, if I had only known you were here!" said Legrand, "but it's so long since I saw you; and how could I foresee that you would pay me a visit this very night of all others? As I was coming home I met Lieutenant G——, from the fort, and, very foolishly, I lent him the bug; so it will be impossible for you to see it until morning. Stay here tonight, and I will send Jup down for it at sunrise. It is the loveliest thing in creation!"

"What?—sunrise?"

"Nonsense! no!—the bug. It is of a brilliant gold color—about the size of a large hickory-nut—with two jet black spots near one extremity of the back, and another, somewhat longer, at the other. The *antennae* are—"

"Dey ain't *no* tin in him, Massa Will, I keep a tellin' on you," here interrupted Jupiter; "de bug is a goole-bug, solid, ebery bit of him, inside and all, sep him wing—never feel half so hebby a bug in my life."

"Well, suppose it is, Jup," replied Legrand, somewhat more earnestly, is seemed to me, than the case demanded, "is that any reason for your letting the birds burn? The color"—here

he turned to me—"is really almost enough to warrant Jupiter's idea. You never saw a more brilliant metallic luster than the scales emit—but of this you cannot judge till tomorrow. In the meantime I can give you some idea of the shape." Saying this, he seated himself at a small table, on which were a pen and ink, but no paper. He looked for some in a drawer, but found none.

"Never mind," said he at length, "this will answer"; and he drew from his waistcoat pocket a scrap of what I took to be very dirty foolscap, and made upon it a rough drawing with the pen. While he did this, I retained my seat by the fire, for I was still chilly. When the design was complete, he handed it to me without rising. As I received it, a loud growl was heard, succeeded by a scratching at the door. Jupiter opened it, and a large Newfoundland, belonging to Legrand, rushed in, leaped upon my shoulders, and loaded me with caresses; for I had shown him much attention during previous visits. When his gambols were over, I looked at the paper, and, to speak the truth, found myself not a little puzzled at what my friend had depicted.

"Well!" I said, after contemplating it for some minutes, "this *is* a strange *scarabaeus,* I must confess: new to me: never saw anything like it before—unless it was a skull, or a death's-head —which it more nearly resembles than anything else that has come under *my* observation."

"A death's-head!" echoed Legrand—"Oh—yes—well, it has something of that appearance upon paper, no doubt. The two upper black spots look like eyes, eh? and the longer one at the bottom like a mouth—and then the shape of the whole is oval."

"Perhaps so," said I; but, Legrand, I fear you are no artist. I must wait until I see the beetle itself, if I am to form any idea of its personal appearance."

"Well, I don't know," said he, a little nettled. "I draw tolerably—*should* do it at least—have had good masters, and flatter myself that I am not quite a blockhead."

"But, my dear fellow, you are joking, then," said I, "this is a very passable *skull*—indeed, I may say that it is a very *excellent* skull, according to the vulgar notions about such specimens of physiology—and your *scarabaeus* must be the queerest *scarabaeus* in the world if it resembles it. Why, we may get up a very thrilling bit of superstition upon this hint. I presume you will call the bug *Scarabaeus caput hominis,* or something of that kind—there are many similar titles in the Natural Histories. But where are the *antennae* you spoke of?"

"The *antennae!*" said Legrand, who seemed to be getting unaccountably warm upon the subject; "I am sure you must see the *antennae.* I made them as distinct as they are in the original insect, and I presume that is sufficient."

"Well, well," I said, "perhaps you have—still I don't see them"; and I handed him the paper without additional remark, not wishing to ruffle his temper; but I was much surprised at the turn affairs had taken; his ill humor puzzled me—and, as for the drawing of the beetle, there were positively *no antennae* visible, and the whole *did* bear a very close resemblance to the ordinary cuts of a death's-head.

He received the paper very peevishly, and was about to crumple it, apparently to throw it in the fire, when a casual glance at the design seemed suddenly to rivet his attention. In an instant his face grew violently red—in another as excessively pale. For some minutes he continued to scrutinize the drawing minutely where he sat. At length he arose, took a candle from the table, and proceeded to seat himself upon a sea-chest in the farthest corner of the room. Here again he made an anxious examination of the paper; turning it in all directions. He said nothing, however, and his conduct greatly astonished me; yet I thought it prudent not to exacerbate the growing moodiness of his temper by any comment. Presently he took from his coat pocket a wallet, placed the paper carefully in it, and deposited both in a writing desk, which he locked. He now grew more composed in his demeanor; but his original air of enthusiasm had quite disappeared. Yet he seemed not so much sulky as abstracted. As the evening wore away he become more and more absorbed in reverie, from which no sallies of mine could arouse him. It had been my intention to pass the night at the hut, as I had frequently done before, but, seeing my host in this mood, I deemed it proper to take leave. He did not press me to remain, but, as I departed, he shook my hand with even more than his usual cordiality.

It was about a month after this (and during the interval I had seen nothing of Legrand) when I received a visit, at Charleston, from his man, Jupiter. I had never seen the good old negro look so dispirited, and I feared that some serious disaster had befallen my friend.

"Well, Jup," said I, "what is the matter now?—how is your master?"

"Why, to speak de troof, massa, him not so berry well as mought be."

"Not well! I am truly sorry to hear it. What does he complain of?"

"Dar! dat's it—him nebber 'plain of notin'—but him berry sick for all dat."

"Very sick, Jupiter!—why didn't you say so at once? Is he confined to bed?"

"No, dat he ain't!—he ain't 'find'd nowhar—dat's just whar de shoe pinch—my mind is got to be berry hebby bout poor Massa Will."

"Jupiter, I should like to understand what it is you are talking about. You say your master is sick. Hasn't he told you what ails him?"

"Why, massa, 'tain't worf while for me to git mad bout de matter—Massa Will say noffin at all ain't de matter wid him—but den what make him go about looking dis here way, wid he head down and he soldiers up, and as white as a gose? And den he keep a syphon all de time—"

"Keeps a what, Jupiter?"

"Keeps a syphon wid de figgurs on de slate—de queerest figgurs I ebber did see. Ise gittin' to be skeered, I tell you. Hab for to keep mighty tight eye pon him 'noovers. Todder day he gib me slip 'fore de sun up and was gone de whole ob de blessed day. I had a big stick ready cut for to gib him d——d good beating when he did come—but Ise sich a fool dat I hadn't de heart arter all—he look so berry poorly."

"Eh?—what?—ah yes!—upon the whole I think you had better not be too severe with the poor fellow—don't flog him, Jupiter—he can't very well stand it—but can you form no idea of what has occasioned this illness, or rather this change of conduct? Has anything unpleasant happened since I saw you?"

"No massa, dey ain't bin noffin onpleasant *since* den—'twas *'fore* den I'm feared—'twas de berry day you was dare."

"How? what do you mean?"

"Why, massa, I mean de bug—dare now."

"The what?"

"De bug—I'm berry sartain dat Massa Will bin bit somewhere bout de head by dat goole bug."

"And what cause have you, Jupiter, for such a supposition?"

"Claws enuff, massa, and mouff, too. I neber did see such a d——d bug—he kick and he bite ebery ting what cum near him. Massa Will cotch him fuss, but had for to let him go 'gin mighty quick, I tell you—den was de time he must ha' got de bite. I didn't like de look ob de bug mouff, myself, nohow, so I wouldn't take hold ob him wid my finger, but I cotch him wid a piece ob paper I found. I rap him up in de paper and stuff piece ob it in he mouff—dat was de way."

"And you think, then, that your master was really bitten by the beetle, and that the bite made him sick?"

"I don't tink noffin about it—I nose it. What make him dream 'bout de goole so much, if 'tain't cause he bit by de goole bug? Ise heard 'bout dem goole bugs 'fore dis."

"But how do you know he dreams about gold?"

"How I know? why cause he talk about it in he sleep—dat's how I nose."

"Well, Jup, perhaps you are right; but to what fortunate circumstance am I to attribute the honor of a visit from you today?"

"What de matter, massa?"

"Did you bring any message from Mr. Legrand?"

"No, massa, I bring dis here 'pissel"; and here Jupiter handed me a note which ran thus:

"My Dear—

"Why have I not seen you for so long a time? I hope you have not been so foolish as to take offense, at any little *brusquerie* of mine; but no, that is improbable.

"Since I saw you I have had great cause for anxiety. I have something to tell you, yet scarcely know how to tell it, or whether I should tell it at all.

"I have not been quite well for some days past, and poor old Jup annoys me, almost beyond endurance, by his well-meant attentions. Would you believe it?—he had prepared a huge stick, the other day, with which to chastise me for giving him the slip, and spending the day, *solus,* among the hills on the mainland. I verily believe that my ill looks alone saved me a flogging.

"I have made no addition to my cabinet since we met.

"If you can, in any way, make it convenient, come over with Jupiter. *Do* come. I wish to see you *tonight,* upon business of importance. I assure you that it is of the *highest* importance.

"Ever yours,

"William Legrand."

There was something in the tone of this note which gave me great uneasiness. Its whole style differed materially from that of Legrand. What could he be dreaming of? What new crotchet possessed his excitable brain? What "business of the highest importance" could *he* possibly have to transact? Jupiter's account of him boded no good. I dreaded lest the continued pressure of misfortune had, at length, fairly unsettled the reason of my friend. Without a moment's hesitation, therefore, I prepared to accompany the negro.

Upon reaching the wharf, I noticed a scythe and three spades, all apparently new, lying in the bottom of the boat in which we were to embark.

"What is the meaning of all this, Jup?" I inquired.

"Him syfe, massa, and spade."

"Very true; but what are they doing here?"

"Him de syfe and de spade what Massa Will sis 'pon my buying for him in de town, and de debbil's own lot of money I had to gib for em."

"But what, in the name of all that is mysterious, is your 'Massa Will' going to do with scythes and spades?"

"Dat's more dan *I* know, and debbil take me if I don't b'lieve 'tis more dan he know, too. But it's all cum ob de bug."

Finding that no satisfaction was to be obtained of Jupiter, whose whole intellect seemed to be absorbed by "de bug," I now stepped into the boat and made sail. With a fair and strong breeze we soon ran into the little cove to the northward of Fort Moultrie, and a walk of some two miles brought us to the hut. It was about three in the afternoon when we arrived. Legrand had been awaiting us in eager expectation. He grasped my hand with a nervous *empressement* which alarmed me and strengthened the suspicions already entertained. His countenance was pale even to ghastliness, and his deep-set eyes glared with unnatural luster. After some inquiries respecting his health, I asked him, not knowing what better to say, if he had yet obtained the *scarabaeus* from Lieutenant G——.

"Oh, yes," he replied, coloring violently, "I got it from him the next morning. Nothing should tempt me to part with that *scarabaeus*. Do you know that Jupiter is quite right about it?"

"In what way?" I asked, with a sad foreboding at heart.

"In supposing it to be a bug of *real gold*." He said this with an air of profound seriousness, and I felt inexpressibly shocked.

"This bug is to make my fortune," he continued, with a trimphant smile, "to reinstate me in my family possessions. Is it any wonder, then, that I prize it? Since Fortune has thought fit to bestow it upon me, I have only to use it properly and I shall arrive at the gold of which it is the index. Jupiter, bring me that *scarabaeus!*"

"What! de bug, massa! I'd rubber not go fer trubble dat bug—you mus' git him for your own self." Hereupon Legrand arose, with a grave and stately air, and brought me the beetle from a glass case in which it was enclosed. It was a beautiful *scarabaeus*, and, at that time, unknown to naturalists—of course a great prize in a scientific point of view. There were two round black spots near one extremity of the back, and a long one near the other. The scales were exceedingly hard and glossy, with all the appearance of burnished gold. The weight of the insect was very remarkable, and, taking all things into consideration, I could hardly blame Jupiter for this opinion respecting it; but what to make of Legrand's agreement with that opinion, I could not, for the life of me, tell.

"I sent for you," said he, in a grandiloquent tone, when I had completed my examination of the beetle, "I sent for you, that I might have your counsel and assistance in furthering the views of Fate and of the bug—"

"My dear Legrand," I cried, interrupting him, "you are certainly unwell, and had better use some little precautions. You shall go to bed, and I will remain with you a few days, until you get over this. You are feverish and—"

"Feel my pulse," said he.

I felt it, and, to say the truth, found not the slightest indication of fever.

"But you may be ill and yet have no fever. Allow me this once to prescribe for you. In the first place, go to bed. In the next—"

"You are mistaken," he interposed, "I am as well as I can expect to be under the excitement which I suffer. If you really wish me well, you will relieve this excitement."

"And how is this to be done?"

"Very easily. Jupiter and myself are going upon an expedition into the hills, upon the mainland, and, in this expedition, we shall need the aid of some person in whom we can confide. You are the only one we can trust. Whether we succeed or fail, the excitement which you now perceive in me will be equally allayed."

"I am anxious to oblige you in any way," I replied; "but do you mean to say that this infernal beetle has any connection with your expedition into the hills?"

"It has."

"Then, Legrand, I can become a party to no such absurd proceeding."

"I am sorry—very sorry—for we shall have to try it by ourselves."

"Try it by yourselves! The man is surely mad!—but stay! how long do you propose to be absent?"

"Probably all night. We shall start immediately, and be back, at all events, by sunrise."

"And will you promise me, upon your honor, that when this freak of yours is over, and the bug business (good God!) settled to your satisfaction, you will then return home and follow my advice implicitly, as that of your physician?"

"Yes; I promise; and now let us be off, for we have no time to lose."

With a heavy heart I accompanied my friend. We started about four o'clock—Legrand, Jupiter, the dog, and myself. Jupiter had with him the scythe and spades—the whole of which he insisted upon carrying—more through fear, it seemed to me, of trusting either of the implements within reach of his master, than from any excess of industry or complaisance. His demeanor was dogged in the extreme, and "dat d——d bug" were the sole words which escaped his lips during the journey. For my own part, I had charge of a couple of dark lanterns, while Legrand contented himself with the *scarabaeus,* which he carried attached to the end of a bit of whipcord; twirling it to and fro, with the air of a conjurer, as he went. When I observed this last, plain evidence of my friend's aberration of mind, I could scarcely refrain from tears. I thought it best, however, to humor his fancy, at least for the present, or until I could adopt some more energetic measures with a chance of success. In the meantime I endeavored, but all in vain, to sound him in regard to the object of the expedition. Having succeeded in inducing me to accompany him, he seemed unwilling to hold conversation upon any topic of minor importance, and to all my questions vouchsafed no other reply than "we shall see!"

We crossed the creek at the head of the island by means of a skiff, and, ascending the high grounds on the shore of the mainland, proceeded in a northwesterly direction, through a tract of the country excessively wild and desolate, where no trace of a human footstep was to be seen. Legrand led the way with decision; pausing only for an instant, here and there, to consult what appeared to be certain landmarks of his own contrivance upon a former occasion.

In this manner we journeyed for about two hours, and the sun was just setting when we entered a region infinitely more dreary than any yet seen. It was a species of tableland, near the summit of an almost inaccessible hill, densely wooded from base to pinnacle, and interspersed with huge crags that appeared to lie loosely upon the soil, and in many cases were prevented from precipitating themselves into the valleys below, merely by the support of the trees against which they reclined. Deep ravines, in various directions, gave an air of still sterner solemnity to the scene.

The natural platform to which we had clambered was thickly overgrown with brambles, through which we soon discovered that it would have been impossible to force our way but for the scythe; and Jupiter, by direction of his master, proceeded to clear for us a path to the foot of an enormously tall tulip-tree, which stood, with some eight or ten oaks, upon the level, and far surpassed them all, and all other trees which I had then ever seen, in the beauty of its foliage and form, in the wide spread of its branches, and in the general majesty of its appearance. When we reached this tree, Legrand turned to Jupiter, and asked him if he thought he could climb it. The old man seemed a little staggered by the question, and for some moments made no reply. At length he approached the huge trunk, walked slowly around it, and examined it with minute attention. When he had completed his scrutiny, he merely said,

"Yes, massa, Jup climb any tree he ebber see in he life."

"Then up with you as soon as possible, for it will soon be too dark to see what we are about."

"How far mus go up, massa?" inquired Jupiter.

"Get up the main trunk first, and then I will tell you which way to go—and here—stop! take this beetle with you."

"De bug, Massa Will!—de goole bug!" cried the negro, drawing back in dismay—"what for mus' tote de bug way up de tree?—d——n if I do!"

"If you are afraid, Jup, a great big negro like you, to take hold of a harmless little dead beetle, why you can carry it up by this string—but, if you do not take it up with you in some way, I shall be under the necessity of breaking your head with this shovel."

"What de matter now, massa?" said Jup, evidently shamed into compliance; "always want for to raise fuss wid ole nigger. Was only funnin anyhow. *Me* feered de bug!—what I keer for de bug!" Here he took cautiously hold of the extreme end of the string, and, maintaining the insect as far from his person as circumstances would permit, prepared to ascend the tree.

In youth, the tulip-tree, or *Liriodendron tulipifera,* the most magnificent of American foresters, has a trunk peculiarly smooth, and often rises to a great height without lateral branches; but, in its riper age, the bark becomes gnarled and uneven, while many short limbs make their appearance on the stem. Thus the difficulty of ascension, in the present case, lay more in semblance than in reality. Embracing the huge cylinder, as closely as possible, with his arms and knees, seizing with his hands some projections, and resting his naked toes upon others, Jupiter, after one or two narrow escapes from falling, at length wriggled himself into the first great fork, and seemed to consider the whole business as virtually accomplished. The *risk* of the achievement was, in fact, now over, although the climber was some sixty or seventy feet from the ground.

"Which way mus' go now, Massa Will?" he asked.

"Keep up the largest branch—the one on this side," said Legrand. The negro obeyed him promptly, and apparently with but little trouble; ascending higher and higher, until no glimpse of his squat figure could be obtained through the dense foliage which enveloped it. Presently his voice was heard in a sort of halloo.

"How much fudder is got for go?"

"How high up are you?" asked Legrand.

"Ebber so fur," replied the negro; "can see de sky fru de top ob de tree."

"Never mind the sky, but attend to what I say. Look down the trunk and count the limbs below you on this side. How many limbs have you passed?"

"One, two, tree, four, fibe—I done pass fibe big limbs, massa, 'pon dis side."

"Then go one limb higher."

In a few minutes the voice was heard again, announcing that the seventh limb was attained.

"Now, Jup," cried Legrand, evidently much excited, "I want you to work your way out upon that limb as far as you can. If you see anything strange, let me know."

By this time what little doubt I might have entertained of my poor friend's insanity, was put finally at rest. I had no alternative but to conclude him stricken with lunacy, and I became seriously anxious about getting him home.

While I was pondering upon what was best to be done, Jupiter's voice was again heard.

"Mos feerd for to ventur 'pon dis limb berry far—'tis dead limb putty much all de way."

"Did you say it was a *dead* limb, Jupiter?" cried Legrand in a quavering voice.

"Yes, massa, him dead as de door-nail—done up for sartain—done departed dis here life."

"What in the name of heaven shall I do?" asked Legrand, seemingly in the greatest distress.

"Do!" said I, glad of an opportunity to interpose a word, "Why, come home and go to bed. Come now! that's a fine fellow. It's getting late, and besides, you remember your promise."

"Jupiter," cried he, without heeding me in the least, "do you hear me?"

"Yes, Massa Will, hear you ebber so plain."

"Try the wood with your knife, and see if it is *very* rotten."

"Him rotten, massa, sure nuff," replied the negro in a few

moments, "but not so berry rotten as mought be. Mought ventur out leetle way 'pon de limb by myself, dat's true."

"By yourself!—what do you mean?"

"Why, I mean de bug. 'Tis *berry* hebby bug. Spose I drop him down fuss, and den de limb won't break wid just de weight ob one nigger."

"You infernal scoundrel!" cried Legrand, apparently much relieved, "what do you mean by telling me such nonsense as that? As sure as you let that beetle fall I'll break your neck. Look here, Jupiter! do you hear me?"

"Yes, massa, needn't hollo at poor nigger dat style."

"Well! now listen!—if you will venture out on the limb as far as you think safe, and not let go the beetle, I'll make you a present of a silver dollar as soon as you get down."

"I'm gwine, Massa Will—deed I is," replied the negro very promptly—"mos' out to the eend now."

"Out to the end!" here fairly screamed Legrand. "Do you say you are out to the end of that limb?"

"Soon be to de eend, massa—o-o-o-o-oh! Lor-gol-a-marcy! what *is* dis here 'pon de tree?"

"Well!" cried Legrand, highly delighted. "What is it?"

"Why 'tain't noffin but a skull—somebody bin lef' him head up de tree, and de crows gone gobble ebery bit ob de meat off."

"A skull, you say!—very well!—how is it fastened to the limb?—what holds it on?"

"Sure nuff, massa; mus' look. Why dis berry curous sarcumstance, 'pon my word—dar's a great big nail in de skull, what fastens ob it on to de tree."

"Well, now, Jupiter, do exactly as I tell you—do you hear?"

"Yes, massa."

"Pay attention, then!—find the left eye of the skull."

"Hum! hoo! dat's good! why dar ain't no eye lef' at all."

"Curse your stupidity! do you know your right hand from your left?"

"Yes, I nose dat—nose all about dat—'tis my lef' hand what I chops de wood wid."

"To be sure! you are left-handed; and your left eye is on the same side as your left hand. Now, I suppose, you can find the left eye of the skull, or the place where the left eye has been. Have you found it?"

Here was a long pause. At length the negro asked,

"Is de lef' eye of de skull 'pon de same side as de lef' hand of de skull, too?—cause de skull ain't got not a bit ob a hand at all—nebber mind! I got de lef' eye now—here de lef' eye! what mus do wid it?"

"Let the beetle drop through it, as far as the string will reach—but be careful and not let go your hold of the string."

"All dat done, Massa Will; mighty easy ting for to put de bug fru de hole—look out for him dar below!"

During this colloquy no portion of Jupiter's person could be seen; but the beetle, which he had suffered to descend, was now visible at the end of the string, and glistened, like a globe of burnished gold, in the last rays of the setting sun, some of which still faintly illumined the eminence upon which we stood. The *scarabaeus* hung quite clear of any branches, and, if allowed to fall, would have fallen at our feet. Legrand immediately took the scythe, and cleared with it a circular space, three or four yards in diameter, just beneath the insect, and, having accomplished this, ordered Jupiter to let go the string and come down from the tree.

Driving a peg, with great nicety, into the ground, at the precise spot where the beetle fell, my friend now produced from his pocket a tape-measure. Fastening one end of this at that point of the trunk of the tree which was nearest the peg, he unrolled it till it reached the peg, and thence farther unrolled it, in the direction already established by the two points of the tree and the peg, for the distance of fifty feet—Jupiter clearing away the brambles with the scythe. At the spot thus attained a second peg was driven, and about this, as a center, a rude circle, about four feet in diameter, described. Taking now a spade himself, and giving one to Jupiter and one to me, Legrand begged us to set about digging as quickly as possible.

To speak the truth, I had no especial relish for such amusement at any time, and, at that particular moment, would most willingly have declined it; for the night was coming on, and I felt much fatigued with the exercise already taken; but I saw no mode of escape, and was fearful of disturbing my poor friend's equanimity by a refusal. Could I have depended, indeed, upon Jupiter's aid, I would have had no hesitation in attempting to get the lunatic home by force; but I was too well assured of the old negro's disposition, to hope that he would assist me, under any circumstances, in a personal contest with his master. I made no doubt that the latter had been infected with some of the innumerable Southern superstitions about money buried, and that his phantasy had received confirmation by the finding of the *scarabaeus*, or, perhaps, by Jupiter's obstinacy in maintaining it to be "a bug of real gold." A mind disposed to lunacy would readily be led away by such suggestions—especially if chiming in with favorite preconceived ideas—and then I called to mind the poor fellow's speech about the beetle's being "the index of his fortune." Upon the whole, I was sadly vexed and puzzled, but, at length, I concluded to make a virtue of necessity—to dig with a good will, and thus the sooner to convince the visionary, by ocular demonstration, of the fallacy of the opinions he entertained.

The lanterns having been lit, we all fell to work with a zeal worthy a more rational cause; and, as the glare fell upon our persons and implements, I could not help thinking how picturesque a group we composed, and how strange and suspicious our labors must have appeared to any interloper who, by chance, might have stumbled upon our whereabouts.

We dug very steadily for two hours. Little was said; and our chief embarrassment lay in the yelpings of the dog, who took exceeding interest in our proceedings. He, at length, became so obstreperous that we grew fearful of his giving the alarm to some stragglers in the vicinity—or, rather, this was the apprehension of Legrand—for myself, I should have rejoiced at any interruption which might have enabled me to get the wanderer home. The noise was, at length, very effectually silenced by Jupiter, who, getting out of the hole with a dogged air of deliberation, tied the brute's mouth up with one of his suspenders, and then returned, with a grave chuckle, to his task.

When the time mentioned had expired, we had reached a depth of five feet, and yet no signs of any treasure became manifest. A general pause ensued, and I began to hope that the farce was at an end. Legrand, however, although evidently much disconcerted, wiped his brow thoughtfully and recommenced. We had excavated the entire circle of four feet diameter, and now we slightly enlarged the limit, and went to the farther depth of two feet. Still nothing appeared. The gold-seeker, whom I sincerely pitied, at length clambered from the pit, with the bitterest disappointment imprinted upon every feature, and proceeded, slowly and reluctantly, to put on his coat, which he had thrown off at the beginning of his labor. In the meantime I made no remark. Jupiter, at a signal from his master, began to gather up his tools. This done, and the dog having been unmuzzled, we turned in profound silence towards home.

We had taken perhaps a dozen steps in this direction, when, with a loud oath, Legrand strode up to Jupiter and seized him by the collar. The astonished negro opened his eyes and mouth to the fullest extent, let fall the spades, and fell upon his knees.

"You scoundrel," said Legrand, hissing out the syllables from between his clenched teeth—"you infernal black villain!—speak, I tell you—answer me this instant, without prevarication!—which—which is your left eye?"

"Oh, my golly, Massa Will! ain't dis here my lef' eye for sartain?" roared the terrified Jupiter, placing his hand upon his *right* organ of vision, and holding it there with a desperate pertinacity, as if in immediate dread of his master's attempt at a gouge.

"I thought so!—I knew it!—hurrah!" vociferated Legrand, letting the negro go, and executing a series of curvets and caracols, much to the astonishment of his valet, who, arising from his knees, looked, mutely, from his master to myself, and then from myself to his master.

"Come! we must go back," said the latter, "the game's not up yet"; and he again led the way to the tulip-tree.

"Jupiter," said he, when we reached its foot, "come here! Was the skull nailed to the limb with the face outward, or with the face to the limb?"

"De face was out, massa, so dat de crows could get at de eyes good, widout any trouble."

"Well, then, was it this eye or that through which you let the beetle fall?"—here Legrand touched each of Jupiter's eyes.

" 'Twas dis eye, massa—de lef' eye—jis as you tell me," and here it was his right eye that the negro indicated.

"That will do—we must try again."

Here my friend, about whose madness I now saw, or fancied that I saw, certain indications of method, removed the peg which marked the spot where the beetle fell, to a spot about three inches to the westward of its former position. Taking, now, the tape-measure from the nearest point of the trunk to the peg, as before, and continuing the extension in a straight line to the distance of fifty feet, a spot was indicated, removed, by several yards, from the point at which we had been digging.

Around the new position a circle, somewhat larger than in the former instance, was now described, and we again set to work with the spades. I was dreadfully weary, but scarcely understanding what had occasioned the change in my thoughts, I felt no longer any great aversion from the labor imposed. I had become most unaccountably interested—nay, even excited. Perhaps there was something, amid all the extravagant demeanor of Legrand—some air of forethought, or of deliberation, which impressed me. I dug eagerly, and now and then caught myself actually looking, with something that very much resembled expectation, for the fancied treasure, the vision of which had demented my unfortunate companion. At a period when such vagaries of thought most fully possessed me, and when we had been at work perhaps an hour and a half, we were again interrupted by the violent howlings of the dog. His uneasiness, in the first instance, had been, evidently, but the result of playfulness or caprice, but he now assumed a bitter and serious tone. Upon Jupiter's again attempting to muzzle him, he made furious resistance, and leaping into the hole, tore up the mould frantically with his claws. In a few seconds he had uncovered a mass of human bones, forming two complete skeletons, intermingled with several buttons of metal, and what appeared to be the dust of decayed woolen. One or two strokes of a spade upturned the blade of a large Spanish knife, and, as we dug farther, three or four loose pieces of gold and silver coin came to light.

At sight of these the joy of Jupiter could scarcely be restrained, but the countenance of his master wore an air of extreme disappointment. He urged us, however, to continue our exertions, and the words were hardly uttered when I stumbled and fell forward, having caught the toe of my boot in a large ring of iron that lay half buried in the loose earth.

We now worked in earnest, and never did I pass ten minutes of more intense excitement. During this interval we had fairly unearthed an oblong chest of wood, which, from its perfect preservation, and wonderful hardness, had plainly been subjected to some mineralizing process—perhaps that of the bichloride of mercury. This box was three feet and a half long, three feet broad, and two and a half feet deep. It was firmly secured by bands of wrought iron, riveted, and forming a kind of trellis-work over the whole. On each side of the chest, near the top, were three rings of iron—six in all—by means of which a firm hold could be obtained by six persons. Our utmost united endeavors served only to disturb the coffer very slightly in its bed.

We at once saw the impossibility of removing so great a weight. Luckily, the sole fastenings of the lid consisted of two sliding bolts. These we drew back—trembling and panting with anxiety. In an instant, a treasure of incalculable value lay gleaming before us. As the rays of the lanterns fell within the pit, there flashed upwards, from a confused heap of gold and of jewels, a glow and a glare that absolutely dazzled our eyes.

I shall not pretend to describe the feelings with which I gazed. Amazement was, of course, predominant. Legrand appeared exhausted with excitement, and spoke very few words. Jupiter's countenance wore, for some minutes, as deadly a pallor as it is possible, in the nature of things, for any negro's visage to assume. He seemed stupefied—thunderstricken. Presently he fell upon his knees in the pit, and, burying his naked arms up to the elbows in gold, let them there remain, as if enjoying the luxury of a bath. At length, with a deep sigh, he exclaimed, as if in a soliloquy,

"And dis all cum ob de goole bug! de putty goole bug! de poor little goole bug, what I bossed in dat sabage kind ob style! Ain't you shamed ob yourself, nigger?—answer me dat!"

It became necessary, at last, that I should arouse both master and valet to the expediency of removing the treasure. It was growing late, and it behooved us to make exertion, that we might get everything housed before daylight. It was difficult to say what should be done; and much time was spent in deliberation—so confused were the ideas of all. We, finally, lightened the box by removing two thirds of its contents, when we were enabled, with some trouble, to raise it from the hole. The articles taken out were deposited among the brambles, and the dog left to guard them, with strict orders from Jupiter neither, upon any pretense, to stir from the spot, nor to open his mouth until our return. We then hurriedly made for home with the chest; reaching the hut in safety, but after excessive toil, at one o'clock in the morning. Worn out as we were, it was not in human nature to do more just then. We rested until two, and had supper; starting for the hills immediately afterwards, armed with three stout sacks, which, by good luck, were upon the premises. A little before four we arrived at the pit, divided the remainder of the booty, as equally as might be, among us, and, leaving the holes unfilled, again set out for the hut, at which, for the second time, we deposited our golden burthens, just as the first streaks of the dawn gleamed from over the tree-tops in the East.

We were now thoroughly broken down; but the intense excitement of the time denied us repose. After an unquiet slumber of some three or four hours' duration, we arose, as if by pre-concert, to make examination of our treasure.

The chest had been full to the brim, and we spent the whole day, and the greater part of the next night, in a scrutiny of its contents. There had been nothing like order or arrangement. Everything had been heaped in promiscuously. Having assorted all with care, we found ourselves possessed of even vaster wealth than we had at first supposed. In coin there was rather more than four hundred and fifty thousand dollars—estimating the value of the pieces, as accurately as we could, by the tables of the period. There was not a particle of silver. All was gold of antique date and of great variety—French, Spanish, and German money, with a few English guineas, and some counters, of which we had never seen specimens before. There were several very large and heavy coins, so worn that we could make nothing of their inscriptions. There was no American money. The value of the jewels we found more difficulty in estimating. There were diamonds—some of them exceedingly large and fine—a hundred and ten in all, and not one of them small; eighteen rubies of remarkable brilliancy—three hundred and ten emeralds, all very beautiful; and twenty-one sapphires, with an opal. These stones had all been broken from their settings and thrown loose in the chest. The settings themselves, which we picked out from among the other gold, appeared to have been beaten up with hammers, as if to prevent identification. Besides all this, there was a vast quantity of solid gold ornaments—nearly two hundred massive finger and ear rings—rich chains—thirty of these, if I remember—eighty-three very large and heavy crucifixes—fine gold censers of great value—a prodigious golden punch-bowl, ornamented with richly chased vine-leaves and Bacchanalian figures; with two sword-handles exquisitely embossed, and many other smaller articles which I cannot recollect. The weight of these valuables exceeded three hundred and fifty pounds avoirdupois; and in this estimate I have not included one hundred and ninety-seven superb gold watches; three of the number being worth each five hundred dollars, if one. Many of them were very old, and as time keepers valueless; the works having suffered, more or less, from corrosion—but all were richly jeweled and in cases of great worth. We estimated the entire contents of the chest, that night, at a million and a half of dollars; and, upon the subsequent disposal of the trinkets and jewels (a few being retained for our own use), it was found that we had greatly undervalued the treasure.

When, at length, we had concluded our examination, and the intense excitement of the time had, in some measure, subsided, Legrand, who saw that I was dying with impatience for a solution of this most extraordinary riddle, entered into a full detail of all the circumstances connected with it.

"You remember," said he, "the night when I handed you the rough sketch I had made of the *scarabaeus*. You recollect also, that I became quite vexed at you for insisting that my drawing resembled a death's-head. When you first made this assertion I thought you were jesting; but afterwards I called to mind the peculiar spots on the back of the insect, and admitted to myself that your remark had some little foundation in fact. Still, the sneer at my graphic powers irritated me—for I am considered a good artist—and, therefore, when you handed me the scrap of parchment, I was about to crumple it up and throw it angrily into the fire."

"The scrap of paper, you mean," said I.

"No; it had much of the appearance of paper, and at first I supposed it to be such, but when I came to draw upon it, I discovered it, at once, to be a piece of very thin parchment. It was quite dirty, you remember. Well, as I was in the very act of crumpling it up, my glance fell upon the sketch at which you had been looking, and you may imagine my astonishment when I perceived, in fact, the figure of a death's-head just where, it seemed to me, I had made the drawing of the beetle. For a moment I was too much amazed to think with accuracy. I knew that my design was very different in detail from this—although there was a certain similarity in general outline. Presently I took a candle, and seating myself at the other end of the room, proceeded to scrutinize the parchment more closely. Upon turning it over, I saw my own sketch upon the reverse, just as I had made it. My first idea, now, was mere surprise at the really remarkable similarity of outline—at the singular coincidence involved in the fact, that unknown to me, there should have been a skull upon the other side of the parchment, immediately beneath my figure of the *scarabaeus,* and that this skull, not only in outline, but in size, should so closely resemble my drawing. I say the singularity of this coincidence absolutely stupefied me for a time. This is the usual effect of such coincidences. The mind struggles to establish a connection—a sequence of cause and effect—and, being unable to do so, suffers a species of temporary paralysis. But, when I recovered from this stupor, there dawned upon me gradually a conviction which startled me even far more than the coincidence. I began distinctly, positively, to remember that there had been *no* drawing on the parchment when I made my sketch of the *scarabaeus.* I became perfectly certain of this; for I recollected turning up first one side and then the other, in search of the cleanest spot. Had the skull been then there, of course I could not have failed to notice it. Here was indeed a mystery which I felt it impossible to explain; but, even at that early moment, there seemed to glimmer, faintly, within the most remote and secret chamber of my intellect, a glow-worm-like conception of that truth which last night's adventure brought to so magnificent a demonstration. I arose at once, and putting the parchment securely away, dismissed all further reflection until I should be alone.

"When you had gone, and when Jupiter was fast asleep, I betook myself to a more methodical investigation of the affair. In the first place I considered the manner in which the parchment had come into my possession. The spot where we discovered the *scarabaeus* was on the coast of the mainland, about a mile eastward of the island, and but a short distance above high water mark. Upon my taking hold of it, it gave me a sharp bite, which caused me to let it drop. Jupiter, with his accustomed caution, before seizing the insect, which had flown towards him, looked about him for a leaf, or something of that nature, by which to take hold of it. It was at this moment that his eyes, and mine also, fell upon the scrap of parchment, which I then supposed to be paper. It was lying half buried in the sand, a corner sticking up. Near the spot where we found it, I observed the remnants of what appeared to have been a ship's long boat. The wreck seemed to have been there for a very great while; for the resemblance to boat timbers could scarcely be traced.

"Well, Jupiter picked up the parchment, wrapped the beetle in it, and gave it to me. Soon afterwards we turned to go home, and on the way met Lieutenant G——. I showed him the insect, and he begged me to let him take it to the fort. On my consenting, he thrust it forthwith into his waistcoat pocket, without the parchment in which it had been wrapped, and which I had continued to hold in my hand during its inspection. Perhaps he dreaded my changing my mind, and thought it best to make sure of the prize at once—you know how enthusiastic he is on all subjects connected with Natural History. At the same time, without being conscious of it, I must have deposited the parchment in my own pocket.

"You remember that when I went to the table, for the purpose of making a sketch of the beetle, I found no paper where it was usually kept. I looked in the drawer, and found none there. I searched my pockets, hoping to find an old letter—and then my hand fell upon the parchment. I thus detail the precise mode in which it came into my possession; for the circumstances impressed me with peculiar force.

"No doubt you will think me fanciful—but I had already established a kind of *connection*. I had put together two links of a great chain. There was a boat lying on a sea-coast, and not far from the boat was a parchment—*not a paper*—with a skull depicted on it. You will, of course, ask 'where is the connection?' I reply that the skull, or death's-head, is the well-known emblem of the pirate. The flag of the death's head is hoisted in all engagements.

"I have said that the scrap was parchment, and not paper. Parchment is durable—almost imperishable. Matters of little moment are rarely consigned to parchment; since, for the mere ordinary purposes of drawing or writing, it is not nearly so well adapted as paper. This reflection suggested some meaning—some relevancy—in the death's-head. I did not fail to observe, also, the *form* of the parchment. Although one of its corners had been, by some accident, destroyed, it could be seen that the original form was oblong. It was just such a slip, indeed, as might have been chosen for a memorandum—for a record of something to be long remembered and carefully preserved."

"But," I interposed, "you say that the skull was *not* upon the parchment when you made the drawing of the beetle. How then do you trace any connection between the boat and the skull—since this latter, according to your own admission, must have been designed (God only knows how or by whom) at some period subsequent to your sketching the *scarabaeus*?"

"Ah, hereupon turns the whole mystery; although the secret, at this point, I had comparatively little difficulty in solving. My steps were sure, and could afford but a single result. I reasoned, for example, thus: When I drew the *scarabaeus,* there was no skull apparent on the parchment. When I had completed the drawing, I gave it to you, and observed you narrowly until you returned it. *You,* therefore, did not design the skull, and no one else was present to do it. Then it was not done by human agency. And nevertheless it was done.

"At this stage of my reflections I endeavored to remember, and *did* remember, with entire distinctness, every incident which occurred about the period in question. The weather was chilly (oh, rare and happy accident!) and a fire was blazing on the hearth. I was heated with exercise and sat near the table. You, however, had drawn a chair close to the chimney. Just as I placed the parchment in your hand, and as you were in the act of inspecting it, Wolf, the Newfoundland, entered, and leaped upon your shoulders. With you left hand you caressed him and kept him off, while your right, holding the parchment, was permitted to fall listlessly between your knees, and in close proximity to the fire. At one moment I thought the blaze had caught it, and was about to caution you, but, before I could speak, you had withdrawn it, and were engaged in its examination. When I considered all these particulars, I doubted not for a moment that *heat* had been the agent in bringing to light, on the parchment, the skull which I saw designed on it. You are well aware that chemical preparations exist, and have existed time out of mind, by means of which it is possible to write on either paper or vellum, so that the characters shall become visible only when subjected to the action of fire. Zaffre, digested in *aqua regia*, and diluted with four times its weight of water, is sometimes employed; a green tint results. The regulus of cobalt, dissolved in spirit of nitre, gives a red. These colors disappear at longer or shorter intervals after the material written on cools, but again become apparent upon the re-application of heat.

"I now scrutinized the death's-head with care. Its outer edges—the edges of the drawing nearest the edge of the vellum—were far more *distinct* than the others. It was clear that the action of the caloric had been imperfect or unequal. I immediately kindled a fire, and subjected every portion of the parchment to a glowing heat. At first, the only effect was the strengthening of the faint lines in the skull; but, on persevering in the experiment, there became visible, at the corner of the slip, diagonally opposite to the spot in which the death's-head was delineated, the figure of what I at first supposed to be a goat. A closer scrutiny, however, satisfied me that it was intended for a kid."

"Ha! ha!" said I, "to be sure I have no right to laugh at you—a million and a half of money is too serious a matter for mirth—but you are not about to establish a third link in your chain—you will not find any especial connection between your pirates and a goat—pirates, you know, have nothing to do with goats; they appertain to the farming interest."

"But I have just said that the figure was *not* that of a goat."

"Well, a kid then—pretty much the same thing."

"Pretty much, but not altogether," said Legrand. "You may have heard of one *Captain* Kidd. I at once looked on the figure of the animal as a kind of punning or hieroglyphical signature. I say signature; because its position on the vellum suggested this idea. The death's-head at the corner diagonally opposite, had, in the same manner, the air of a stamp, or seal. But I was sorely put out by the absence of all else—of the body to my imagined instrument—of the text for my context."

"I presume you expected to find a letter between the stamp and the signature."

"Something of that kind. The fact is, I felt irresistibly impressed with a presentiment of some vast good fortune impending. I can scarcely say why. Perhaps, after all, it was rather a desire than an actual belief—but do you know that

Jupiter's silly words, about the bug being of solid gold, had a remarkable effect on my fancy? And then the series of accidents and coincidences—these were so *very* extraordinary. Do you observe how mere an accident it was that these events should have occurred on the *sole* day of all the year in which it has been, or may be, sufficiently cool for fire, and that without the fire, or without the intervention of the dog at the precise moment in which he appeared, I should never have become aware of the death's-head, and so never the possessor of the treasure?"

"But proceed—I am all impatience."

"Well; you have heard, of course, the many stories current—the thousand vague rumors afloat about money buried, somewhere on the Atlantic coast, by Kidd and his associates. These rumors must have had some foundation in fact. And that the rumors have existed so long and so continuously could have resulted, it appeared to me, only from the circumstance of the buried treasure still *remaining* entombed. Had Kidd concealed his plunder for a time, and afterwards reclaimed it, the rumors would scarcely have reached us in their present unvarying form. You will observe that the stories told are all about money-seekers, not about money-finders. Had the pirate recovered his money, there the affair would have dropped. It seemed to me that some accident—say the loss of a memorandum indicating its locality—had deprived him of the means of recovering it, and that this accident had become known to his followers, who otherwise might never have heard that treasure had been concealed at all, and who, busying themselves in vain, because unguided, attempts to regain it, had given first birth, and then universal currency, to the reports which are now so common. Have you ever heard of any important treasure being unearthed along the coast?"

"Never."

"But that Kidd's accumulations were immense, is well known. I took it for granted, therefore, that the earth still held them; and you will scarcely be surprised when I tell you that I felt a hope, nearly amounting to certainty, that the parchment so strangely found, involved a lost record of the place of deposit."

"But how did you proceed?"

"I held the vellum again to the fire, after increasing the heat; but nothing appeared. I now thought it possible that the coating of dirt might have something to do with the failure; so I carefully rinsed the parchment by pouring warm water over it, and, having done this, I placed it in a tin pan, with the skull downwards, and put the pan upon a furnace of lighted charcoal. In a few minutes, the pan having become thoroughly heated, I removed the slip, and, to my inexpressible joy, found it spotted, in several places, with what appeared to be figures arranged in lines. Again I placed it in the pan, and suffered it to remain another minute. On taking it off, the whole was just as you see it now."

Here Legrand, having re-heated the parchment, submitted it to my inspection. The following characters were rudely traced, in a red tint, between the death's-head and the goat:

53‡‡†305))6*;4826)4‡.)4‡);806*;48†8¶60))85;(;]8
*);:‡*8†83(88)5*†;46(;88*96*?;8)*‡(;485);5*†2:*
‡(;4956*2(5*-4)8¶8*;4069285);)6†8)4‡‡;1(‡9;4808
1;8:8‡1;48†85;4)485†528806*81(‡9;48;(88;4(‡?34;4
8)4‡;161;:188;‡?;

"But," said I, returning him the slip, "I am as much in the dark as ever. Were all the jewels of Golconda awaiting me on my solution of this enigma, I am quite sure that I should be unable to earn them."

"And yet," said Legrand, "the solution is by no means so difficult as you might be led to imagine from the first hasty inspection of the characters. These characters, as any one might readily guess, form a cipher—that is to say, they convey a meaning; but then, from what is known of Kidd, I could not suppose him capable of constructing any of the more abstruse cryptographs. I made up my mind, at once, that this was of a simple species, such, however, as would appear, to the crude intellect of the sailor, absolutely insoluble without the key."

"And you really solved it?"

"Readily; I have solved others of an abstruseness ten thousand times greater. Circumstances, and a certain bias of mind, have led me to take interest in such riddles, and it may well be doubted whether human ingenuity can construct an enigma of the kind which human ingenuity may not, by proper application, resolve. In fact, having once established connected and legible characters, I scarcely gave a thought to the mere difficulty of developing their import.

"In the present case—indeed in all cases of secret writing—the first question regards the *language* of the cipher; for the principles of solution, so far, especially, as the more simple ciphers are concerned, depend upon, and are varied by, the genius of the particular idiom. In general, there is no alternative but experiment (directed by probabilities) of every tongue known to him who attempts the solution, until the true one be attained. But, with the cipher now before us, all difficulty is removed by the signature. The pun on the word 'Kidd' is appreciable in no other language than the English. But for this consideration I should have begun my attempts with the Spanish and French, as the tongues in which a secret of this kind would most naturally have been written by a pirate of the Spanish main. As it was, I assumed the cryptograph to be English.

"You observe there are no divisions between the words. Had there been divisions, the task would have been comparatively easy. In such case I should have commenced with a collation and analysis of the shorter words, and, had a word of a single letter occurred, as is most likely (*a* or *I*, for example,) I should have considered the solution as assured. But, there being no division, my first step was to ascertain the predominant letters, as well as the least frequent. Counting all, I constructed a table, thus:

Of the character	8	there are 33.
	;	there are 26.
	4	there are 19.
	‡)	there are 16.
	*	there are 13.
	5	there are 12.
	6	there are 11.
	† 1	there are 8.
	0	there are 6.
	9 2	there are 5.

: 3	there are	4.
?	there are	3.
¶	there are	2.
] - .	there are	1.

"Now, in English, the letter which most frequently occurs is *e*. Afterwards, the succession runs thus: *a o i d h n r s t u y c f g l m w b k p q x z*. *E*, however, predominates so remarkably that an individual sentence of any length is rarely seen, in which it is not the prevailing character.

"Here, then, we have, in the very beginning, the ground-work for something more than a mere guess. The general use which may be made of the table is obvious—but, in this particular cipher, we shall only very partially require its aid. As our predominant character is 8, we will commence by assuming it as the *e* of the natural alphabet. To verify the supposition, let us observe if the 8 be seen often in couples—for *e* is doubled with great frequency in English—in such words, for example, as 'meet,' 'fleet,' 'speed,' 'seen,' 'been,' 'agree,' &c. In the present instance we see it doubled no less than five times, although the cryptograph is brief.

"Let us assume 8, then, as *e*. Now, of all *words* in the language, 'the' is most usual; let us see, therefore, whether there are not repetitions of any three characters, in the same order of collocation, the last of them being 8. If we discover repetitions of such letters, so arranged, they will most probably represent the word 'the.' On inspection, we find no less than seven such arrangements, the characters being ;48. We may, therefore, assume that the semicolon represents *t*, that 4 represents *h*, and that 8 represents *e*—the last being now well confirmed. Thus a great step has been taken.

"But, having established a single word, we are enabled to establish a vastly important point; that is to say, several commencements and terminations of other words. Let us refer, for example, to the last instance but one, in which the combination ;48 occurs—not far from the end of the cipher. We know that the semicolon immediately ensuing is the commencement of a word, and, of the six characters succeeding this 'the,' we are cognizant of no less than five. Let us set these characters down, thus, by the letters we know them to represent, leaving a space for the unknown—

t eeth.

"Here we are enabled, at once, to discard the '*th*,' as forming no portion of the word commencing with the first *t;* since, by experiment of the entire alphabet for a letter adapted to the vacancy we perceive that no word can be formed of which this *th* can be a part. We are thus narrowed into

t ee,

and, going through the alphabet, if necessary, as before, we arrive at the word 'tree' as the sole possible reading. We thus gain another letter, *r,* represented by (, with the words 'the tree' in juxtaposition.

"Looking beyond these words, for a short distance, we again see the combination ;48, and employ it by way of *termination* to what immediately precedes. We have thus this arrangement:

the tree;4(‡?34 the,

or, substituting the natural letters, where known, it reads thus:

the tree thr‡?3h the.

"Now, if, in place of the unknown characters, we leave blank spaces, or substitute dots, we read thus:

the tree thr . . . h the,

when the word 'through' makes itself evident at once. But this discovery gives us three new letters, *o, u* and *g,* represented by ‡ ? and 3.

"Looking now, narrowly, through the cipher for combinations of known characters, we find, not very far from the beginning, this arrangement,

83(88, or egree,

which, plainly, is the conclusion of the word 'degree,' and gives us another letter, *d,* represented by †.

"Four letters beyond the word 'degree,' we perceive the combination

;46(;88*

"Translating the known characters, and representing the unknown by dots, as before, we read thus:

th.rtee.

an arrangement immediately suggestive of the word 'thirteen,' and again furnishing us with two new characters, *i* and *n*, represented by 6 and *.

"Referring, now, to the beginning of the cryptograph, we find the combination,

53‡‡†.

"Translating, as before, we obtain

.good,

which assures us that the first letter is *A*, and that the first two words are 'A good.'

"To avoid confusion, it is now time that we arrange our key, as far as discovered, in a tabular form. It will stand thus:

5 represents a
† represents d
8 represents e
3 represents g
4 represents h
6 represents i
* represents n
‡ represents o
(represents r
; represents t.

"We have, therefore, no less than ten of the most important letters represented, and it will be unnecessary to proceed with the details of the solution. I have said enough to convince you that ciphers of this nature are readily soluble, and to give you some insight into the *rationale* of their development. But be assured that the specimen before us appertains to the very simplest species of cryptograph. It now only remains to give you the full translation of the characters upon the parchment, as unriddled. Here it is:

" '*A good glass in the bishop's hostel in the devil's seat twenty-one degrees and thirteen minutes northeast and by north main branch seventh limb east side shoot from the left eye of the death's head a bee line from the tree through the shot fifty feet out.'"*

"But," said I, "the enigma seems still in as bad a condition as ever. How is it possible to extort a meaning from all this jargon about 'devil's seats,' 'death's-head,' and 'bishop's hotels'?"

"I confess," replied Legrand, "that the matter still wears a serious aspect, when regarded with a casual glance. My first endeavor was to divide the sentence into the natural division intended by the cryptographist."

"You mean, to punctuate it?"

"Something of that kind."

"But how was it possible to effect this?"

"I reflected that it had been a *point* with the writer to run his words together without division, so as to increase the difficulty of solution. Now, a not over-acute man, in pursuing such an object, would be nearly certain to overdo the matter. When, in the course of his composition, he arrived at a break in his subject which would naturally require a pause, or a point, he would be exceedingly apt to run his characters, at this place, more than usually close together. If you will observe the MS., in the present instance, you will easily detect five such cases of unusual crowding. Acting on this hint, I made the division thus:

"'*A good glass in the Bishop's hostel in the Devil's seat—twenty-one degrees and thirteen minutes—northeast and by north—main branch seventh limb east side—shoot from the left eye of the death's-head—a bee-line from the tree through the shot fifty feet out.*'"

"Even this division," said I, "leaves me still in the dark."

"It left me also in the dark," replied Legrand, "for a few days; during which I made diligent inquiry, in the neighborhood of Sullivan's Island, for any building which went by the name of the 'Bishop's Hotel'; for, of course, I dropped the obsolete word 'hostel.' Gaining no information on the subject, I was on the point of extending my sphere of search, and proceeding in a more systematic manner, when, one morning, it entered my head, quite suddenly, that this 'bishop's hostel' might have some reference to an old family, of the name of Bessop, which, time out of mind, had held possession of an ancient manor-house, about four miles to the northward of the Island. I accordingly went over to the plantation, and reinstituted my inquiries among the older negroes of the place. At length one of the most aged of the women said that she had heard of such a place as *Bessop's Castle,* and thought that she could guide me to it, but that it was not a castle, nor a tavern, but a high rock.

"I offered to pay her well for her trouble, and, after some demur, she consented to accompany me to the spot. We found it without much difficulty, when, dismissing her, I proceeded to examine the place. The 'castle' consisted of an irregular assemblage of cliffs and rocks—one of the latter being quite remarkable for its height as well as for its insulated and artificial appearance. I clambered to its apex, and then felt much at a loss as to what should be next done.

"While I was busied in reflection, my eyes fell upon a narrow ledge in the eastern face of the rock, perhaps a yard below the summit on which I stood. This ledge projected about eighteen inches, and was not more than a foot wide, while a niche in the cliff just above it gave it a rude resemblance to one of the hollow-backed chairs used by our ancestors. I made no doubt that here was the 'devil's seat' alluded to in the MS., and now I seemed to grasp the full secret of the riddle.

"The 'good glass,' I knew, could have reference to nothing but a telescope; for the word 'glass' is rarely employed in any other sense by seamen. Now here, I at once saw, was a telescope to be used, and a definite point of view, *admitting no variation,* from which to use it. Nor did I hesitate to believe that the phrases, 'twenty-one degrees and thirteen minutes,' and 'northeast and by north,' were intended as directions for the leveling of the glass. Greatly excited by these discoveries, I hurried home, procured a telescope, and returned to the rock.

"I let myself down to the ledge, and found that it was impossible to retain a seat on it unless in one particular position. This

fact confirmed my preconceived idea. I proceeded to use the glass. Of course, the 'twenty-one degrees and thirteen minutes' could allude to nothing but elevation above the visible horizon, since the horizontal direction was clearly indicated by the words, 'northeast and by north.' This latter direction I at once established by means of a pocket-compass; then, pointing the glass as nearly at an angle of twenty-one degrees of elevation as I could do it by guess, I moved it cautiously up or down, until my attention was arrested by a circular rift or opening in the foliage of a large tree that overtopped its fellows in the distance. In the center of this rift I perceived a white spot, but could not, at first, distinguish what it was. Adjusting the focus of the telescope, I again looked, and now made it out to be a human skull.

"On this discovery I was so sanguine as to consider the enigma solved; for the phrase 'main branch, seventh limb, east side,' could refer only to the position of the skull on the tree, while 'shoot from the left eye of the death's-head' admitted, also, of but one interpretation, in regard to a search for buried treasure. I perceived that the design was to drop a bullet from the left eye of the skull, and that a bee-line, or, in other words, a straight line, drawn from the nearest point of the trunk through 'the shot' (or the spot where the bullet fell) and thence extended to a distance of fifty feet, would indicate a definite point—and beneath this point I thought it at least *possible* that a deposit of value lay concealed."

"All this," I said, "is exceedingly clear, and, although ingenious, still simple and explicit. When you left the Bishop's Hotel, what then?"

"Why, having carefully taken the bearings of the tree, I turned homewards. The instant that I left 'the devil's seat,' however, the circular rift vanished; nor could I get a glimpse of it afterwards, turn as I would. What seems to me the chief ingenuity in this whole business, is the fact (for repeated experiment has convinced me it *is* a fact) that the circular opening in question is visible from no other attainable point of view than that afforded by the narrow ledge on the face of the rock.

"In this expedition to the 'Bishop's Hotel' I had been attended by Jupiter, who had, no doubt, observed, for some weeks past, the abstraction of my demeanor, and took especial care not to leave me alone. But, on the next day, getting up very early, I contrived to give him the slip, and went into the hills in search of the tree. After much toil I found it. When I came home at night my valet proposed to give me a flogging. With the rest of the adventure I believe you are as well acquainted as myself."

"I suppose," said I, "you missed the spot, in the first attempt at digging, through Jupiter's stupidity in letting the bug fall through the right instead of through the left eye of the skull."

"Precisely. This mistake made a difference of about two inches and a half in the 'shot'—that is to say, in the position of the peg nearest the tree; and had the treasure been *beneath* the 'shot,' the error would have been of little moment; but 'the shot,' together with the nearest point of the tree, were merely

two points for the establishment of a line of direction; of course the error, however trivial in the beginning, increased as we proceeded with the line, and by the time we had gone fifty feet, threw us quite off the scent. But for my deep-seated convictions that treasure was here somewhere actually buried, we might have had all our labor in vain."

"I presume the fancy of *the skull*—of letting fall a bullet through the skull's eye—was suggested to Kidd by the piratical flag. No doubt he felt a kind of poetical consistency in recovering his money through this ominous insignium."

"Perhaps so; still I cannot help thinking that common sense had quite as much to do with the matter as poetical consistency. To be visible from the devil's seat, it was necessary that the object, if small, should be *white;* and there is nothing like your human skull for retaining and even increasing its whiteness under exposure to all vicissitudes of weather."

"But your grandiloquence, and your conduct in swinging the beetle—how excessively odd! I was sure you were mad. And why did you insist on letting fall the bug, instead of a bullet, from the skull?"

"Why, to be frank, I felt somewhat annoyed by your evident suspicions touching my sanity, and so resolved to punish you quietly, in my own way, by a little bit of sober mystification. For this reason I swung the beetle, and for this reason I let it fall from the tree. An observation of yours about its great weight suggested the latter idea."

"Yes, I perceive; and now there is only one point which puzzles me. What are we to make of the skeletons found in the hole?"

"That is a question I am no more able to answer than yourself. There seems, however, only one plausible way of accounting for them—and yet it is dreadful to believe in such atrocity as my suggestion would imply. It is clear that Kidd—if Kidd indeed secreted this treasure, which I doubt not—it is clear that he must have had assistance in the labor. But, the worst of this labor concluded, he may have thought it expedient to remove all participants in his secret. Perhaps a couple of blows with a mattock were sufficient, while his coadjutors were busy in the pit; perhaps it required a dozen—who shall tell?"

The Gold Bug *was first published in 1843 in the Philadelphia Dollar Magazine.*

The Devil Fish

BY JULES VERNE

Illustrations by Kurt Wiese

Long before the true submarine became a reality, Jules Verne gave the world the fabulous story of Captain Nemo and his underwater craft. The breathtaking adventures of the crew and passengers continue to hold readers spellbound, a lasting tribute to the rich imagination and genuine scientific background of the highly ingenious French author.

FOR several days the *Nautilus* kept off from the American coast. Evidently it did not wish to risk the tides of the Gulf of Mexico, or of the sea of the Antilles. April 16th, we sighted Martinique and Guadeloupe from a distance of about thirty miles. I saw their tall peaks for an instant. The Canadian, who counted on carrying out his projects in the Gulf, by either landing, or hailing one of the numerous boats that coast from one island to another, was quite disheartened. Flight would have been quite practicable, if Ned Land had been able to take possession of the boat without the Captain's knowledge. But in the open sea it could not be thought of. The Canadian, Conseil, and I, had a long conversation on this subject. For six months we had been prisoners on board the *Nautilus*. We had travelled 17,000 leagues; and, as Ned Land said, there was no reason why it should not come to an end. We could hope for nothing from the Captain of the *Nautilus*, but only from ourselves. Besides, for some time past he had become graver, more retired, less sociable. He seemed to shun me. I met him rarely. Formerly, he was pleased to explain the submarine marvels to me; now,

From *Twenty Thousand Leagues under the Sea*, by Jules Verne.

he left me to my studies, and came no more to the saloon. What change had come over him? For what cause? For my part, I did not wish to bury with me my curious and novel studies. I had now the power to write the true book of the sea; and this book, sooner or later, I wished to see daylight. Then again, in the water of the Antilles, ten yards below the surface of the waters, by the open panels, what interesting products I had to enter on my daily notes! There were, among other zoophytes, those known under the name of physalis pelagica, a sort of large oblong bladder, with mother-of-pearl rays, holding out their membranes to the wind, and letting their blue tentacles float like threads of silk; charming medusæ to the eye, real nettles to the touch, that distil a corrosive fluid. There were also annelides, a yard and a half long, furnished with a pink horn, and with 1700 locomotive organs, that wind through the waters, and throw out in passing all the light of the solar spectrum. There were, in the fish category, some Malabar rays, enormous gristly things, ten feet long, weighing 600 pounds, the pectoral fin triangular in the midst of a slightly humped back, the eyes fixed in the extremities of the face, beyond the head, and which floated like weft, and looked sometimes like an opaque shutter on our glass window. There were American balistæ, which nature has only dressed in black and white; gobies, with yellow fins and prominent jaw; mackerel sixteen feet long, with short-pointed teeth, covered with small scales, belonging to the albicore species. Then, in swarms, appeared grey mullet, covered with stripes of gold from the head to the tail, beating their resplendent fins, like masterpieces of jewellery, consecrated formerly to Diana, particularly sought after by rich Romans, and of which the proverb says, "Whoever takes them does not eat them." Lastly, pomacanthe dorees, ornamented with emerald bands, dressed in velvet and silk, passed before our eyes like Veronese lords; spurred spari passed with their pectoral fins; clupanodons fifteen inches long, enveloped in their phosphorescent light; mullet beat the sea with their large jagged tails; red vendaces seemed to mow the waves with their showy pectoral fins; and silvery selenes, worthy of their name, rose on the horizon of the waters like so many moons with whitish rays. April 20th, we had risen to a mean height of 1500 yards. The land nearest us then was the archipelago of the Bahamas. There rose high submarine cliffs covered with large weeds, giant laminariæ and fuci, a perfect espalier of hydrophytes worthy of a Titan world. It was about eleven o'clock when Ned Land drew my attention to a formidable pricking, like the sting of an ant, which was produced by means of large seaweeds.

"Well," I said, "these are proper caverns for poulps, and I should not be astonished to see some of these monsters."

"What!" said Conseil; "cuttle-fish, real cuttle-fish, of the cephalopod class?"

"No," I said; "poulps of huge dimensions."

"I will never believe that such animals exist," said Ned.

"Well," said Conseil, with the most serious air in the world; "I remember perfectly to have seen a large vessel drawn under the waves by a cephalopod's arm."

"You saw that?" said the Canadian.

"Yes, Ned."

"With your own eyes?"

"With my own eyes."

"Where, pray, might that be?"

"At St. Malo," answered Conseil.

"In the port?" said Ned, ironically.

"No; in a church," replied Conseil.

"In a church!" cried the Canadian.

"Yes, friend Ned. In a picture representing the poulp in question."

"Good!" said Ned Land, bursting out laughing.

"He is quite right," I said. "I have heard of this picture; but the subject represented is taken from a legend, and you know what to think of legends in the matter of natural history. Besides, when it is a question of monsters, the imagination is apt to run wild. Not only is it supposed that these poulps can draw down vessels, but a certain Olaüs Magnus speaks of a cephalopod a mile long, that is more like an island than an animal. It is also said that the Bishop of Nidros was building an altar on an immense rock. Mass finished, the rock began to walk, and returned to the sea. The rock was a poulp. Another bishop, Pontoppidan, speaks also of a poulp on which a regiment of cavalry could manœuvre. Lastly, the ancient naturalists speak of monsters whose mouths were like gulfs, and which were too large to pass through the Straits of Gibraltar."

"But how much is true of these stories?" asked Conseil.

"Nothing, my friends; at least of that which passes the limit of truth to get to fable or legend. Nevertheless, there must be some ground for the imagination of the storytellers. One cannot deny that poulps and cuttle-fish exist of a large species, inferior, however, to the cetaceans. Aristotle has stated the dimensions of a cuttle-fish as five cubits, or nine feet two inches. Our fishermen frequently see some that are more than four feet long. Some skeletons of poulps are preserved in the museums of Trieste and Montpelier, that measure two yards in length. Besides, according to the calculations of some naturalists, one of these animals, only six feet long, would have tentacles twenty-seven feet long. That would suffice to make a formidable monster."

"Do they fish for them in these days?" asked Ned.

"If they do not fish for them, sailors see them at least. One of my friends, Captain Paul Bos of Havre, has often affirmed that he met one of these monsters, of colossal dimensions, in the Indian seas. But the most astonishing fact, and which does not permit the denial of the existence of these gigantic animals, happened some years ago, in 1861."

"What is the fact?" asked Ned Land.

"This is it. In 1861, to the north-east of Teneriffe, very nearly in the same latitude we are in now, the crew of the despatch-boat *Alector* perceived a monstrous cuttle-fish swimming in the waters. Captain Bouguer went near to the animal, and attacked it with harpoons and guns, without much success, for balls and harpoons glided over the soft flesh. After several fruitless attempts, the crew tried to pass a slip-knot round the body of the mollusc. The noose slipped as far as the caudal fins, and there stopped. They tried then to haul it on board, but its weight was so considerable that the tightness of the cord separated the tail from the body, and, deprived of this ornament, he disappeared under the water."

"Indeed! is that a fact?"

"An indisputable fact, my good Ned. They proposed to name this poulp 'Bouguer's cuttle-fish.' "

"What length was it?" asked the Canadian.

"Did it not measure about six yards?" said Conseil, who, posted at the window, was examining again the irregular windings of the cliff.

"Precisely," I replied.

"Its head," rejoined Conseil, "was it not crowned with eight tentacles, that beat the water like a nest of serpents?"

"Precisely."

"Had not its eyes, placed at the back of its head, considerable development?"

"Yes, Conseil."

"And was not its mouth like a parrot's beak?"

"Exactly, Conseil."

"Very well! no offence to master," he replied, quietly; "if this is not Bouguer's cuttle-fish, it is, at least, one of its brothers."

I looked at Conseil. Ned hurried to the window.

"What a horrible beast!" he cried.

I looked in my turn, and could not repress a gesture of disgust. Before my eyes was a horrible monster, worthy to figure in the legends of the marvellous. It was an immense cuttle-fish, being eight yards long. It swam crossways in the direction of the *Nautilus* with great speed, watching us with its enormous staring green eyes. Its eight arms, or rather feet, fixed to its head, that have given the name of cephalopod to these animals, were twice as long as its body, and were twisted like the furies' hair. One could see the 250 air-holes on the inner side of the tentacles. The monster's mouth, a horned beak like a parrot's, opened and shut vertically. Its tongue, a horned substance, furnished with several rows of pointed teeth, came out quivering from this veritable pair of shears. What a freak of nature, a bird's beak on a mollusc! Its spindle-like body formed a fleshy mass that might weigh 4000 to 5000 lbs.; the varying colour changing with great rapidity, according to the irritation of the animal, passed successively from livid grey to reddish brown. What irritated this mollusc? No doubt the presence of the *Nautilus,* more formidable than itself, and on which its suckers or its jaws had no hold. Yet, what monsters these poulps are! what vitality the Creator has given them! what vigour in their movements! and they possess three hearts! Chance had brought us in presence of this cuttle-fish, and I did not wish to lose the opportunity of carefully studying this specimen of cephalopods. I overcame the horror that inspired me; and, taking a pencil, began to draw it.

"Perhaps this is the same which the *Alector* saw," said Conseil.

"No," replied the Canadian; "for this is whole, and the other had lost its tail."

"That is no reason," I replied. "The arms and tails of these animals grow on again if broken off; and, in seven years, the tail of Bouguer's cuttle-fish has no doubt had time to grow."

By this time other poulps appeared at the port light. I counted seven. They formed a procession after the *Nautilus,* and I heard their beaks gnashing against the iron hull. I continued my work. These monsters kept in the water with such precision, that they seemed immovable. Suddenly the *Nautilus* stopped. A shock made it tremble in every plate.

"Have we struck anything?" I asked.

"In any case," replied the Canadian, "we shall be free, for we are floating."

The *Nautilus* was floating, no doubt, but it did not move. A minute passed. Captain Nemo, followed by his lieutenant, entered the drawing-room. I had not seen him for some time. He seemed dull. Without noticing or speaking to us, he went to the panel, looked at the poulps, and said something to his lieutenant. The latter went out. Soon the panels were shut. The ceiling was lighted. I went towards the Captain.

"A curious collection of poulps" I said.

"Yes, indeed, Mr. Naturalist," he replied; "and we are going to fight them, man to beast."

I looked at him. I thought I had not heard aright.

"Man to beast?" I repeated.

"Yes, sir. The screw is stopped. I think that the horny jaws of one of the cuttle-fish is entangled in the blades. That is what prevents our moving."

"What are you going to do?"

"Rise to the surface, and slaughter this vermin."

"A difficult enterprise."

"Yes, indeed. The electric bullets are powerless against the soft flesh, where they do not find resistance enough to go off. But we shall attack them with the hatchet."

"And the harpoon, sir," said the Canadian, "if you do not refuse my help."

"I will accept it, Master Land."

"We will follow you," I said, and following Captain Nemo, we went towards the central staircase.

There, about ten men with boarding hatchets were ready for the attack. Conseil and I took two hatchets; Ned Land seized a harpoon. The *Nautilus* had then risen to the surface. One of the sailors, posted on the top ladder-step, unscrewed the bolts of the panels. But hardly were the screws loosed, when the panel rose with great violence, evidently drawn by the suckers of a poulp's arm. Immediately one of these arms slid like a serpent down the opening, and twenty others were above. With one blow of the axe, Captain Nemo cut this formidable tentacle, that slid wriggling down the ladder. Just as we were pressing one on the other to reach the platform, two other arms, lashing the air, came down on the seaman placed before Captain Nemo, and lifted him up with irresistible power. Captain Nemo uttered a cry, and rushed out. We hurried after him.

What a scene! The unhappy man, seized by the tentacle, and fixed to the suckers, was balanced in the air at the caprice of this enormous trunk. He rattled in his throat, he was stifled, he cried, "Help! help!" These words, *spoken in French,* startled me! I had a fellow-countryman on board, perhaps several! That heartrending cry! I shall hear it all my life. The unfortunate man was lost. Who could rescue him from that powerful pressure? However, Captain Nemo had rushed to the poulp, and with one blow of the axe had cut through one arm. His lieutenant struggled furiously against other monsters that crept on the flanks of the *Nautilus.* The crew fought with their axes. The Canadian, Conseil, and I, buried our weapons in the fleshy masses; a strong smell of musk penetrated the atmosphere. It was horrible!

For one instant, I thought the unhappy man, entangled with the poulp, would be torn from its powerful suction. Seven of the eight arms had been cut off. One only wriggled in the air, brandishing the victim like a feather. But just as Captain Nemo and his lieutenant threw themselves on it, the animal ejected a stream of black liquid. We were blinded with it. When the cloud dispersed, the cuttle-fish had disappeared, and my unfortunate countryman with it. Ten or twelve poulps now invaded the platform and sides of the *Nautilus.* We rolled pell-mell into the midst of this nest of serpents, that wriggled on

the platform in the waves of blood and ink. It seemed as though these slimy tentacles sprang up like the hydra's heads. Ned Land's harpoon, at each stroke, was plunged into the staring eyes of the cuttle-fish. But my bold companion was suddenly overturned by the tentacles of a monster he had not been able to avoid.

Ah! how my heart beat with emotion and horror! The formidable beak of a cuttle-fish was open over Ned Land. The unhappy man would be cut in two. I rushed to his succour. But Captain Nemo was before me; his axe disappeared between the two enormous jaws, and, miraculously saved, the Canadian, rising, plunged his harpoon deep into the triple heart of the poulp.

"I owed myself this revenge!" said the Captain to the Canadian.

Ned bowed without replying. The combat had lasted a quarter of an hour. The monsters, vanquished and mutilated, left us at last, and disappeared under the waves. Captain Nemo, covered with blood, nearly exhausted, gazed upon the sea that had swallowed up one of his companions, and great tears gathered in his eyes.

First published in 1870, Twenty Thousand Leagues Under the Sea *rivals* Around the World in Eighty Days *as the most popular of Jules Verne's works.*

Gulliver's Voyage to Lilliput

BY JONATHAN SWIFT

Edited by Padraic Colum

Illustrations by Willy Pogany

Readers have taken such delight for so many years in the entrancing story of the travels of Lemuel Gulliver that many have forgotten the book was originally written as a satire on the follies of the English court of the day and was first published anonymously. When even those being lampooned were highly entertained, Swift acknowledged the work and was accorded a great ovation.

The Author gives some account of himself and family, his first inducements to travel—He is shipwrecked and swims for his life, gets safe on shore in the country of Lilliput, *is made a prisoner and carried up country.*

MY father had a small estate in Nottinghamshire; I was the third of five sons. He sent me to Emanuel College in Cambridge, at fourteen years old, where I resided three years, and applied myself close to my studies; but the charge of maintaining me (although I had a very scanty allowance) being too great for a narrow fortune, I was bound apprentice to Mr. James Bates, an eminent surgeon in London, with whom I continued four years; and my father now and then sending me small sums of money, I laid them out in learning navigation, and other parts of the mathematics, useful to those who intend to travel, as I always believed it would be some time or other my fortune to do. When I left Mr. Bates, I went down to my

father; where, by the assistance of him and my uncle John, and some other relations, I got forty pounds, and a promise of thirty pounds a year to maintain me at Leyden: there I studied physic two years and seven months, knowing it would be useful in long voyages.

Soon after my return from Leyden, I was recommended by my good master, Mr. Bates, to be surgeon to the *Swallow*, Captain Abraham Pannell, commander; with whom I continued three years and a half, making a voyage or two into the Levant, and some other parts. When I came back I resolved to settle in London, to which Mr. Bates, my master, encouraged me, and by him I was recommended to several patients. I took part of a small house in the Old Jury; and being advised to alter my condition, I married Mrs. Mary Burton, second daughter to Mr. Edmund Burton, hosier, in Newgate-street, with whom I received four hundred pounds for a portion.

But, my good master Bates dying in two years after, and I having few friends, my business began to fail; for my conscience would not suffer me to imitate the bad practice of too many among my brethren. Having therefore consulted with my wife, and some of my acquaintance, I determined to go again to sea. I was surgeon successively in two ships, and made several voyages, for six years, to the East and West Indies, by which I got some addition to my fortune. My hours of leisure I spent in reading the best authors, ancient and modern, being always provided with a good number of books; and when I was ashore, in observing the manners and dispositions of the people, as well as learning their language, wherein I had a great facility by the strength of my memory.

The last of these voyages not proving very fortunate, I grew weary of the sea, and intended to stay at home with my wife and family. I removed from the Old Jury to Fetter-Lane, and from thence to Wapping, hoping to get business among the sailors; but it would not turn to account. After three years' expectation that things would mend, I accepted an advantageous offer from Captain William Prichard, master of the *Antelope*, who was making a voyage to the South Sea. We set sail from Bristol, May 4, 1699, and our voyage at first was very prosperous.

It would not be proper, for some reasons, to trouble the reader with the particulars of our adventures in those seas: let it suffice to inform him, that in our passage from thence to the East Indies, we were driven by a violent storm to the northwest of Van Diemen's Land. By an observation, we found ourselves in the latitude of 30 degrees 2 minutes south. Twelve of our crew were dead by immoderate labor, and ill food, the rest were in a very weak condition. On the fifth of November, which was the beginning of summer in those parts, the weather being very hazy, the seamen spied a rock, within half a cable's length of the ship; but the wind was so strong, that we were driven directly upon it, and immediately split. Six of the crew, of whom I was one, having let down the boat into the sea, made a shift to get clear of the ship, and the rock. We rowed, by my computation, about three leagues, till we were able to work no longer, being already spent with labor while we were in the ship. We therefore trusted ourselves to the mercy of the waves, and in about half an hour the boat was overset by a sudden flurry from the north. What became of my companions in the boat, as well as of those who escaped on the rock, or were left in the vessel, I cannot tell; but conclude they were all lost. For my own part, I swam as fortune directed me, and was pushed forward by wind and tide. I often let my legs drop, and could feel no bottom: but when I was almost gone, and able to struggle no longer, I found myself within my depth; and by this time the storm was much abated. The declivity was so small, that I walked near a mile before I got to the shore, which I conjectured was about eight o'clock in the evening. I then advanced forward near half a mile, but could not discover any sign of houses or inhabitants; at least I was in so weak a condition, that I did not observe them. I was extremely tired, and with that, and the heat of the weather, and about half a pint of brandy that I drank as I left the ship, I found myself much inclined to sleep. I lay down on the grass, which was very short and soft, where I slept sounder than ever I remember to have done in my life, and, as I reckoned, about nine hours; for when I awaked, it was just daylight. I attempted to arise, but was not able to stir: for as I happened to lie on my back, I found my arms and legs were strongly fastened on each side of the ground; and my hair, which was long and thick, tied down in the same manner. I likewise felt several slender ligatures across my body, from my arm-pits to my thighs. I could only look upward, the sun began to grow hot, and the light offended my eyes. I heard a confused noise about me, but in the posture I lay, could see nothing except the sky. In a little time I felt something alive moving on my left leg, which advancing gently forward over my breast, came almost up to my chin; when bending my eyes downward as much as I could, I perceived it to be a human creature not six inches high,* with a bow and arrow in his hands, and a quiver at his back. In the meantime, I felt at least forty more of the same kind (as I conjectured) following the first. I was in the utmost astonishment, and roared so loud, that they all ran back in a fright; and some of them, as I was afterwards told, were hurt with the falls they got by leaping from my sides upon the ground. However, they soon returned, and one of them, who ventured so far as to get a full sight of my face, lifting up his hands and eyes by way of admiration, cried out in a shrill, but distinct voice, *Hekinah degul:* the others repeated the same words several times, but then I knew not what they meant: I lay all this while, as the reader may believe, in great uneasiness: at length, struggling to get loose, I had the fortune to break the strings, and wrench out the pegs that fastened my left arm to the ground; for, by lifting it up to my face, I dis-

* The people of Lilliput measure in inches about what a man measures in feet; a person of six inches would be tall among them. Everything in the country is of a size proportional to the inhabitants: horses, wagons, temples, trees, animals are in inches what ours would be in feet.

covered the methods they had taken to bind me, and at the same time with a violent pull, which gave me excessive pain, I a little loosened the strings that tied down by hair on the left side, so that I was just able to turn my head about two inches. But the creatures ran off a second time, before I could seize them; whereupon there was a great shout in a very shrill accent, and after it ceased, I heard one of them cry aloud *Tolgo phonac;* when in an instant I felt about a hundred arrows discharged on my left hand, which pricked me like so many needles; and besides, they shot another flight into the air, as we do bombs in Europe, whereof many, I suppose, fell on my body (though I felt them not), and some on my face, which I immediately covered with my left hand. When this shower of arrows was over, I fell a-groaning with grief and pain, and then striving again to get loose, they discharged another volley larger than the first, and some of them attempted with spears to stick me in the sides; but, by good luck, I had on a buff jerkin, which they could not pierce. I thought it the most prudent method to lie still, and my design was to continue so till night, when, my left hand being already loose, I could easily free myself; and as for the inhabitants, I had reason to believe I might be a match for the greatest armies they could bring against me, if they were all of the same size with him that I saw. But fortune disposed otherwise of me. When the people observed I was quiet, they discharged no more arrows; but, by the noise I heard, I knew their numbers increased; and about four yards from me, over against my right ear, I heard a knocking for above an hour, like that of people at work; when turning my head that way, as well as the pegs and strings would permit me, I saw a stage erected, about a foot and a half from the ground, capable of holding four of the inhabitants, with two or three ladders to mount it: from whence one of them, who seemed to be a person of quality, made me a long speech, whereof I understood not one syllable. But I should have mentioned, that before the principal person began his oration, he cried out three times, *Langro dehul sans* (these words and the former were afterwards repeated and explained to me). Whereupon immediately about fifty of the inhabitants came and cut the strings that fastened the left side of my head, which gave me the liberty of turning it to the right, and of observing the person and gesture of him that was to speak. He appeared to be of middle age, and taller than any of the other three who attended him, whereof one was a page that held up his train, and seemed to be somewhat longer than my middle finger; the other two stood one on each side to support him. He acted every part of an orator, and I could observe many periods of threatenings, and others of promises, pity, and kindness. I answered in a few words, but in the most submissive manner, lifting up my left hand, and both my eyes to the sun, as calling him for a witness; and being almost famished with hunger, having not eaten a morsel for some hours before I left the ship, I found the demands of nature so strong upon me, that I could not forbear showing my impatience (perhaps against the strict rules of decency) by putting my finger frequently on my mouth, to signify that I wanted food. The *Hurgo* (for so they call a great lord, as I afterwards learned) understood me very well. He descended from the stage, and commanded that several ladders should be applied to my sides, on which above a hundred of the inhabitants mounted and walked toward my mouth, laden with baskets full of meat, which had been provided and sent thither by the King's orders, upon the first intelligence he received of me. I observed there was the flesh of several animals, but could not distinguish them by the taste. There were shoulders, legs, and loins, shaped like those of mutton, and very well dressed, but smaller than the wings of a lark. I ate them by two or three at a mouthful, and took three loaves at a time, about the bigness of musket bullets. They supplied me as fast as they could, showing a thousand marks of wonder and astonishment at my bulk and appetite. I then made another sign that I wanted drink. They found by my eating, that a small quantity would not suffice me; and being a most ingenious people, they slung up with great dexterity one of their largest hogsheads, then rolled it towards my hand, and beat out the top; I drank it off at a draught, which I might well do, for it did not hold half a pint,* and tasted like a small wine of

* Our measure would be 1,728 times as great as that of the Lilliputians; half a pint would thus be equivalent to 108 Lilliputian gallons.

Burgundy, but much more delicious. They brought me a second hogshead, which I drank in the same manner, and made signs for more, but they had none to give me. When I had performed these wonders, they shouted for joy, and danced upon my breast, repeating several times as they did at first, *Hekinah degul.* They made me a sign that I should throw down the two hogsheads, but first warning the people below to stand out of the way, crying aloud, *Borach mivola,* and when they saw the vessels in the air, there was an universal shout of *Hekinah degul.* I confess I was often tempted, while they were passing backwards and forwards on my body, to seize forty of fifty of the first that came in my reach, and dash them against the ground. But the remembrance of what I had felt, which probably might not be the worst they could do, and the promise of honor I made them, for so I interpreted my submissive behavior, soon drove out these imaginations. Besides, I now considered myself as bound by the laws of hospitality to a people who had treated me with so much expense and magnificence. However, in my thoughts, I could not sufficiently wonder at the intrepidity of these diminutive mortals, who durst venture to mount and walk upon my body, while one of my hands was at liberty, without trembling at the very sight of so prodigious a creature as I must appear to them. After some time, when they observed that I made no more demands for meat, there appeared before me a person of high rank from his Imperial Majesty. His Excellency, having mounted on the small of my right leg, advanced forwards up to my face, with about a dozen of his retinue. And producing his credentials under the Signet Royal, which he applied close to my eyes, spoke about ten minutes, without any signs of anger, but with a kind of determinate resolution; often pointing forwards, which as I afterwards found, was towards the capital city, about half a mile distant, whither it was agreed by his Majesty in council that I must be conveyed. I answered in few words, but to no purpose, and made a sign with my hand that was loose, putting it to the other (but over his Excellency's head for fear of hurting him or his train) and then to my own head and body, to signify that I desired my liberty. It appeared that he understood me well enough, for he shook his head by way of disapprobation, and held his hand in a posture to show that I must be carried as a prisoner. However, he made other signs to let me understand that I should have meat and drink enough, and very good treatment. Whereupon I once more thought of attempting to break my bonds; but again, when I felt the smart of their arrows, upon my face and hands, which were all in blisters, and many of the darts still sticking in them, and observing likewise that the number of my enemies increased, I gave tokens to let them know that they might do with me what they pleased. Upon this, the *Hurgo* and his train withdrew, with much civility and cheerful countenances. Soon after I heard a general shout, with frequent repetitions of the words, *Peplom selan,* and I felt great numbers of people on my left side relaxing the cords to such a degree, that I was able to turn upon my right side. But before this, they had daubed my face and both my hands with a sort of ointment very pleasant to the smell, which in a few minutes removed all the smart of their arrows. These circumstances, added to the refreshment I had received by their victuals and drink, which were very nourishing, disposed me to sleep. I slept about eight hours, as I was afterwards assured; and it was no wonder, for the physicians, by the Emperor's order, had mingled a sleepy potion in the hogshead of wine.

It seems that upon the first moment I was discovered sleeping on the ground after my landing, the Emperor had early notice of it by an express; and determined in council that I should be tied in the manner I have related (which was done in the night while I slept), that plenty of meat and drink should be sent to me, and a machine prepared to carry me to the capital city.

This resolution perhaps may appear very bold and dangerous, and I am confident would not be imitated by any prince in Europe on the like occasion; however, in my opinion, it was extremely prudent, as well as generous: for supposing these people had endeavored to kill me with their spears and arrows while I was asleep, I should certainly have awaked with the first sense of smart, which might so far have roused my rage and strength, as to have enabled me to break the strings wherewith I was tied; after which, as they were not able to make resistance, so they could expect no mercy.

These people are most excellent mathematicians, and arrived to a great perfection in mechanics, by the countenance and encouragement of the Emperor, who is a renowned patron of learning. This prince hath several machines fixed on wheels, for the carriage of trees and other great weights. He often builds his largest men of war, whereof some are nine foot long, in the woods, where the timber grows, and has them carried on these engines three or four hundred yards to the sea. Five hundred carpenters and engineers were immediately set at work to prepare the greatest engine they had. It was a frame of wood raised three inches from the ground, about seven foot long and four wide, moving upon twenty-two wheels. The shout I heard was upon the arrival of this engine, which it seems set out in four hours after my landing. It was brought parallel to me as I lay. But the principal difficulty was to raise and place me in this vehicle. Eighty poles, each of one foot high, were erected for this purpose, and very strong cords of the bigness of packthread were fastened by hooks to many bandages, which the workmen had girt round my neck, my hands, my body, and my legs. Nine hundred of the strongest men were employed to draw up these cords by many pulleys fastened on the poles, and thus, in less than three hours, I was raised and slung into the engine, and there tied fast. All this I was told, for, while the whole operation was performing, I lay in a profound sleep, by the force of that soporiferous medicine infused into my liquor. Fifteen hundred of the Emperor's largest horses, each about four inches and a half high, were employed to draw me towards the metropolis, which, as I said, was half a mile distant.

About four hours after we began our journey, I awaked by a very ridiculous accident; for the carriage being stopped a while to adjust something that was out of order, two or three of the young natives had the curiosity to see how I looked when I was asleep; they climbed up into the engine, and advancing very softly to my face, one of them, an officer in the guards, put the sharp end of his half-pike a good way up into my left nostril, which tickled my nose like a straw, and made me sneeze violently: whereupon they stole off unperceived, and it was three weeks before I knew the cause of my awaking so suddenly. We made a long march the remaining part of that

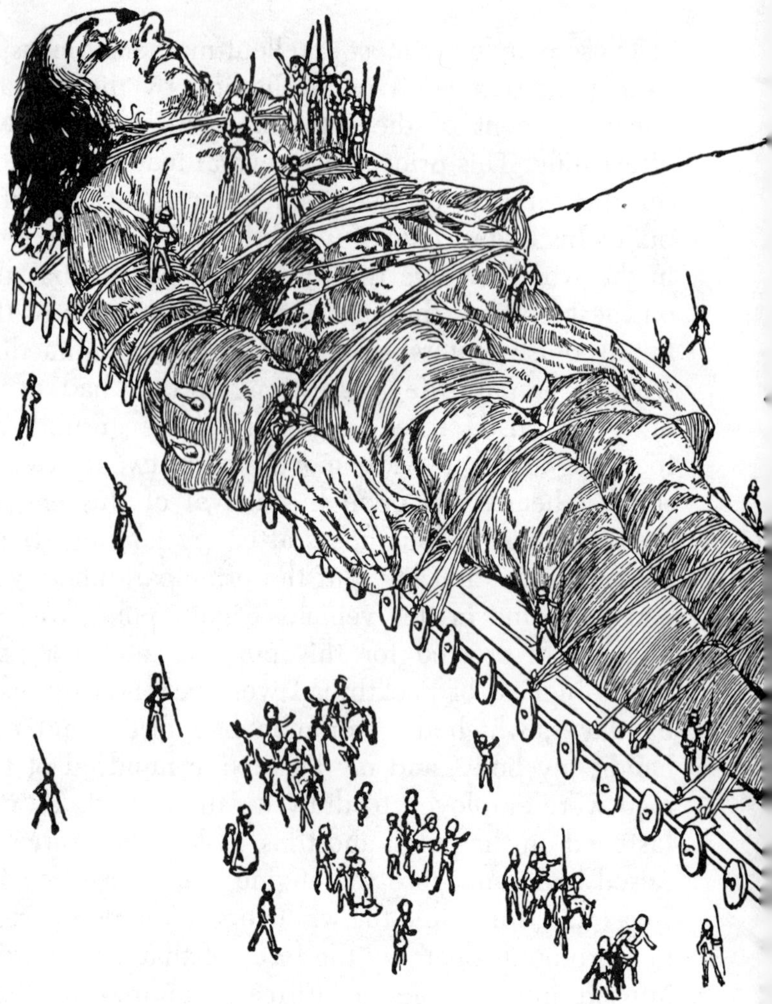

day, and rested at night with five hundred guards on each side of me, half with torches, and half with bows and arrows, ready to shoot me if I should offer to stir. The next morning at sunrise we continued our march and arrived within two hundred yards of the city gates about noon. The Emperor, and all his court, came out to meet us; but his great officers would by no means suffer his Majesty to endanger his person by mounting on my body.

At the place where the carriage stopped, there stood an ancient temple, esteemed to be the largest in the whole kingdom; which having been polluted some years before by an unnatural murder, was, according to the zeal of those people,

looked upon as profane, and therefore had been applied to common uses, and all the ornaments and furniture carried away. In this edifice it was determined I should lodge. The great gate fronting to the north was about four foot high, and almost two foot wide, through which I could easily creep. On each side of the gate was a small window not above six inches from the ground: into that on the left side, the King's smiths conveyed fourscore and eleven chains, like those that hang to a lady's watch in Europe and almost as large, which were locked to my left leg with six and thirty padlocks. Over against this temple, on t'other side of the great highway, at twenty foot distance, there was a turret at least five foot high. Here the Emperor ascended, with many principal lords of his court, to have an opportunity of viewing me, as I was told, for I could not see them. It was reckoned that above a hundred thousand inhabitants came out of the town upon the same errand; and, in spite of my guards, I believe there could not be fewer than ten thousand at several times, who mounted my body by the help of ladders. But a proclamation was soon issued to forbid it upon pain of death. When the workmen found it was impossible for me to break loose, they cut all the strings that bound me; whereupon I rose up, with as melancholy a disposition as ever I had in my life. But the noise and astonishment of the people at seeing me rise and walk, are not to be expressed. The chains that held my left leg were about two yards long, and gave me not only the liberty of walking backwards and forwards in a semi-circle; but, being fixed within four inches of the gate, allowed me to creep in, and lie at my full length in the temple.

The Emperor of Lilliput, *attended by several of the nobility, comes to see the Author in his confinement—The Emperor's person and habit described—Learned men appointed to teach the Author their language—He gains favor by his mild disposition—His pockets are searched, and his sword and pistols taken.*

When I found myself on my feet, I looked about me, and must confess I never beheld a more entertaining prospect. The country round appeared like a continued garden, and the enclosed fields, which were generally forty foot square, resembled so many beds of flowers. These fields were intermingled with woods of half a stang,* and the tallest trees, as I could judge, appeared to be seven foot high. I viewed the town on my left hand, which looked like the painted scene of a city in a theater.

The Emperor was already descended from the tower, and advancing on horseback toward me, which had like to have cost him dear; for the beast, though very well trained, yet wholly unused to such a sight, which appeared as if a mountain moved before him, reared up on his hinder feet: but that

* A stang is a pole or perch; sixteen feet and a half.

prince, who is an excellent horseman, kept his seat, till his attendants ran in, and held the bridle, while his Majesty had time to dismount. When he alighted, he surveyed me round with great admiration, but kept beyond the length of my chain. He ordered his cooks and butlers, who were already prepared, to give me victuals and drink, which they pushed forward in a sort of vehicles upon wheels, till I could reach them. I took these vehicles, and soon emptied them all; twenty of them were filled with meat, and ten with liquor; each of the former afforded me two or three good mouthfuls, and I emptied the liquor of ten vessels, which was contained in earthen vials, into one vehicle, drinking it off at a draught; and so I did with the rest. The Empress, and young Princes of the blood of both sexes, attended by many ladies, sat at some distance in their chairs; but upon the accident that happened to the Emperor's horse, they alighted, and came near his person, which I am now going to describe.

He is taller by almost the breadth of my nail, than any of his court; which alone is enough to strike an awe into the beholders. His features are strong and masculine, with an Austrian lip and arched nose, his complexion olive, his countenance erect, his body and limbs well proportioned, all his motions graceful, and his deportment majestic. He was then past his prime, being twenty-eight years and three quarters old, of which he had reigned about seven, in great felicity, and generally victorious. For the better convenience of beholding him, I lay on my side, so that my face was parallel to his, and he stood but three yards off: however, I have had him since many times in my hand, and therefore cannot be deceived in the description. His dress was very plain and simple, and the fashion of it between the Asiatic and the European: but he had on his head a light helmet of gold, adorned with jewels, and a plume on the crest. He held his sword drawn in his hand, to defend himself, if I should happen to break loose; it was almost three inches long, the hilt and scabbard were gold enriched with diamonds. His voice was shrill, but very clear and articulate, and I could distinctly hear it when I stood up. The ladies and courtiers were all most magnificently clad, so that the spot they stood upon seemed to resemble a petticoat spread on the ground, embroidered with figures of gold and silver. His Imperial Majesty spoke often to me, and I returned answers, but neither of us could understand a syllable. There were several of his priests and lawyers present (as I conjectured by their habits) who were commanded to address themselves to me, and I spoke to them in as many languages as I had the least smattering of, which were High and Low Dutch, Latin, French, Spanish, Italian, and Lingua Franca; but all to no purpose. After about two hours the court retired, and I was left with a strong guard, to prevent the impertinence, and probably the malice of the rabble, who were very impatient to crowd about me as near as they durst, and some of them had the impudence to shoot their arrows at me as I sat on the ground by the door of my house, whereof one very narrowly missed my left eye. But the colonel ordered six of the ringleaders to be seized, and thought no punishment so proper as to deliver them bound into my hands, which some of his soldiers accordingly did, pushing them forward with the butt-ends of their pikes into my reach; I took them all in my right hand, put five of them into my coat-pocket, and as to the sixth, I made a countenance as if I would eat him alive. The poor man squalled terribly, and the colonel and his officers were in much pain, especially when they saw me take out my penknife: but I soon put them out of fear: for, looking mildly, and immediately cutting the strings he was bound with, I set him gently on the ground, and away he ran. I treated the rest in the same manner, taking them one by one out of my pocket, and I observed both the soldiers and people were highly obliged at this mark of my clemency, which was represented very much to my advantage at court.

Toward night I got with some difficulty into my house, where I lay on the ground, and continued to do so about a fortnight; during which time the Emperor gave orders to have a bed prepared for me. Six hundred beds of the common measure were brought in carriages, and worked up in my house; a hundred and fifty of their beds sewn together made up the breadth and length, and these were four double, which however kept me but very indifferently from the hardness of the floor, that was of smooth stone. By the same computation they provided me with sheets, blankets, and coverlets, tolerable enough for one who had been so long inured to hardships as I.

As the news of my arrival spread through the kingdom, it brought prodigious numbers of rich, idle, and curious people to see me; so that the villages were almost emptied, and great neglect of tillage and household affairs must have ensued, if his Imperial Majesty had not provided, by several proclamations and orders of state, against this inconveniency. He directed that those who had already beheld me should return home, and not presume to come within fifty yards of my house without license from court; whereby the secretaries of state got considerable fees.

In the meantime, the Emperor held frequent councils to debate what course should be taken with me; and I was afterwards assured by a particular friend, a person of great quality, who was looked upon to be as much in the secret as any, that the court was under many difficulties concerning me. They apprehended my breaking loose, that my diet would be very expensive, and might cause a famine. Sometimes they determined to starve me, or at least to shoot me in the face and hands with poisoned arrows, which would soon dispatch me; but again they considered that the stench of so large a carcass might produce a plague in the metropolis, and probably spread through the whole kingdom. In the midst of these consultations, several officers of the army went to the door of the great council-chamber; and two of them being admitted, gave an account of my behavior to the six criminals above-mentioned, which made so favorable an impression in the breast of his

Majesty and the whole board, in my behalf, that an Imperial Commission was issued out, obliging all the villages nine hundred yards round the city, to deliver in every morning six beeves, forty sheep, and other victuals for my sustenance; together with a proportionable quantity of bread, and wine, and other liquors; for the due payment of which his Majesty gave assignments upon his treasury. For this prince lives chiefly upon his own demesnes, seldom, except upon great occasions, raising any subsidies upon his subjects, who are bound to attend him in his wars at their own expense.

An establishment was also made of six hundred persons to be my domestics, who had board-wages allowed for their maintenance, and tents built for them very conveniently on each side of my door. It was likewise ordered, that three hundred tailors should make me a suit of clothes after the fashion of the country: that six of his Majesty's greatest scholars should be employed to instruct me in their language: and, lastly, that the Emperor's horses, and those of the nobility, and troops of guards, should be frequently exercised in my sight, to accustom themselves to me.

All these orders were duly put in execution, and in about three weeks I made a great progress in learning their language; during which time, the Emperor frequently honored me with his visits, and was pleased to assist my masters in teaching me. We began already to converse together in some sort; and the first words I learned were to express my desire that he would please give me my liberty, which I every day repeated on my knees. His answer, as I could comprehend it, was that this must be a work of time, not to be thought on without the advice of his council, and that first I must *Lumos kelmin pesso desmar lon Emposo;* that is, swear a peace with him and his kingdom. However, that I should be used with all kindness; and he advised me to acquire, by my patience and discreet behavior, the good opinion of himself and his subjects. He desired I would not take it ill, if he gave orders to certain proper officers to search me; for probably I might carry about me several weapons, which must needs be dangerous things, if they answered the bulk of so prodigious a person. I said, his Majesty should be satisfied, for I was ready to strip myself, and turn up my pockets before him. This I delivered part in words, and part in signs. He replied, that by the laws of the kingdom I must be searched by two of his officers; that he knew this could not be done without my consent and assistance; and he had so good an opinion of my generosity and justice, as to trust their persons in my hands: that whatever they took from me should be returned when I left the country, or paid for at the rate which I would set upon them. I took up the two officers in my hands, put them first into my coat-pockets, and then into every other pocket about me, except my two fobs, and another secret pocket which I had no mind should be searched, wherein I had some little necessaries that were of no consequence to any but myself. In one of my fobs there was a silver watch, and in the other a small quantity of gold in a purse. These gentlemen, having pen, ink, and paper about them, made an exact inventory of everything they saw; and when they had done, desired I would set them down, that they might deliver it to the Emperor. This inventory I afterwards translated into English, and is word for word as follows:

> *Imprimis,* In the right coat-pocket of the Great Man-Mountain (for so I interpret the words *Quinbus Flestrin*) after the strictest search, we found only one great piece of coarse cloth, large enough to be a foot-cloth for your Majesty's chief room of state. In the left pocket we saw a huge silver chest, with a cover of the same metal, which we, the searchers, were not able to lift. We desired it should be opened, and one of us stepping into it, found himself up to the mid leg in a sort of dust, some part whereof flying up to our faces, set us both a-sneezing for several times together. In his right waistcoat-pocket we found a prodigious bundle of white thin substances, folded one over another, about the bigness of three men, tied with a strong cable, and marked with black figures; which we humbly conceive to be writings, every letter almost half as large as the palm of our hands. In the left there was a sort of engine, from the back of which were extended twenty long poles, resembling the pallisados before your Majesty's court: wherewith we conjecture the

Man-Mountain combs his head; for we did not always trouble him with questions, because we found it a great difficulty to make him understand us. In the large pocket on the right side of his middle cover (so I translate the word *ranfu-lo,* by which they meant my breeches) we saw a hollow pillar of iron, about the length of a man, fastened to a strong piece of timber, larger than the pillar; and upon one side of the pillar were huge pieces of iron sticking out, cut into strange figures, which we know not what to make of. In the left pocket another engine of the same kind. In the smaller pocket on the right side, were several round flat pieces of white and red metal, of different bulk; some of the white, which seemed to be silver, were so large and heavy, that my comrade and I could hardly lift them. In the left pocket were two black pillars irregularly shaped: we could not, without difficulty, reach the top of them as we stood at the bottom of his pocket. One of them was covered, and seemed all of a piece: but at the upper end of the other, there appeared a white round substance, about twice the bigness of our heads. Within each of these was enclosed a prodigious plate of steel; which, by our orders, we obliged him to show us, because we apprehended they might be dangerous engines. He took them out of their cases, and told us, that in his own country his practice was to shave his beard with one of these, and cut his meat with the other. There were two pockets which we could not enter: these he called his fobs; they were two large slits cut into the top of his middle cover, but squeezed close by the pressure of his belly. Out of the right fob hung a great silver chain, with a wonderful kind of engine at the bottom. We directed him to draw out whatever was fastened to that chain; which appeared to be a globe, half silver, and half of some transparent metal; for, on the transparent side, we saw certain strange figures circularly drawn, and thought we could touch them, till we found our fingers stopped by that lucid substance. He put this engine to our ears, which made an incessant noise like that of a water-mill. And we conjecture it is either some unknown animal, or the god that he worships; but we are more inclined to the latter opinion, because he assured us (if we understood him right, for he expressed himself very imperfectly) that he seldom did anything without consulting it. He called it his oracle, and said it pointed out the time for every action of his life. From the left fob he took out a net almost large enough for a fisherman, but contrived to open and shut like a purse, and served him for the same use: we found therein several massy pieces of yellow metal, which, if they be real gold, must be of immense value.

Having thus, in obedience to your Majesty's commands, diligently searched all his pockets, we observed a girdle about his waist made of the hide of some prodigious animal; from which, on the left side, hung a sword of the length of five men; and on the right, a bag or pouch divided into two cells, each cell capable of holding three of your Majesty's subjects. In one of these cells were several globes or balls of a most ponderous metal, about the bigness of our heads, and requiring a strong hand to lift them: the other cell contained a heap of certain black grains, but of no great bulk or weight, for we could hold about fifty of them in the palms of our hands.

This is an exact inventory of what we found about the body of the Man-Mountain, who used us with great civility, and due respect to your Majesty's Commission. Signed and sealed on the fourth day of the eighty-ninth moon of your Majesty's auspicious reign.

CLEFRIN FRELOCK, MARSI FRELOCK.

When this inventory was read over to the Emperor, he directed me, although in very gentle terms, to deliver up the several particulars. He first called for my scimitar, which I took out, scabbard and all. In the meantime he ordered three thousand of his choicest troops (who then attended him) to surround me at a distance, with their bows and arrows just ready to discharge: but I did not observe it, for my eyes were wholly fixed upon his Majesty. He then desired me to draw my scimitar, which, although it had got some rust by the sea-water, was in most parts exceeding bright. I did so, and immediately all the troops gave a shout between terror and surprise; for the sun shone clear, and the reflection dazzled their eyes, as I waved the scimitar to and fro in my hand. His Majesty, who is a most magnanimous prince, was less daunted than I could expect; he ordered me to return it into the scabbard, and cast it on the ground as gently as I could, about six foot from the end of my chain. The next thing he demanded, was one of the hollow iron pillars, by which he meant my pocket-pistols. I drew it out, and at his desire, as well as I could, expressed to him the use of it; and charging it only with powder, which, by the closeness of my pouch, happened to escape wetting in the sea (an inconvenience against which all prudent mariners take special care to provide), I first cautioned the Emperor not to be afraid, and then I let it off in the air. The astonishment here was much greater than at the sight of my scimitar. Hundreds fell down as if they had been struck dead; and even the Emperor, although he stood his ground, could not recover himself in some time. I delivered up both my pistols in the same manner, as I had done my scimitar, and then my pouch of powder and bullets; begging him that the former might be kept from fire, for it would kindle with the smallest spark, and blow up his imperial palace into the air. I likewise delivered up my watch, which the Emperor was very curious to see, and commanded two of his tallest yeomen of the guards to bear it on a pole upon their shoulders, as draymen in England do a barrel of ale. He was amazed at the continual noise it made, and the motion of the minute-hand, which he could easily discern; for their sight is much more acute than ours: and asked the opinions of his learned men about him, which were various and remote, as the reader may well imagine without my repeating; although indeed I could not very perfectly understand them. I then gave up my silver and copper money, my purse, with nine large pieces of gold, and some smaller ones; my knife and razor, my comb and silver snuff-box, my handkerchief and journal-book. My scimitar, pistols, and pouch, were conveyed in carriages to his Majesty's stores; but the rest of my goods were returned to me.

I had, as I before observed, one private pocket which escaped their search, wherein there was a pair of spectacles (which I sometimes use for the weakness of my eyes), a pocket perspective, and several other little conveniences; which being of no consequence to the Emperor, I did not think myself bound in honor to discover, and I apprehended they might be lost or spoiled if I ventured them out of my possession.

The Author diverts the Emperor, and his nobility of both sexes, in a very uncommon manner—The diversions of the court of Lilliput *described—The Author has his liberty granted him upon certain conditions.*

My gentleness and good behavior had gained so far on the Emperor and his court, and indeed upon the army and people in general, that I began to conceive hopes of getting my liberty in a short time. I took all possible methods to cultivate this favorable disposition. The natives came by degrees to be less apprehensive of any danger from me. I would sometimes lie down, and let five or six of them dance on my hand. And at last the boys and girls would venture to come and play at hide and seek in my hair. I had now made a good progress in understanding and speaking their language. The Emperor had a mind one day to entertain me with several of the country shows, wherein they exceed all nations I have known, both for dexterity and magnificence. I was diverted with none so much as that of the rope-dancers, performed upon a slender white thread, extended about two foot, and twelve inches from the ground. Upon which I shall desire liberty, with the reader's patience, to enlarge a little.

This diversion is only practised by those persons who are candidates for great employments, and high favor, at court. They are trained in this art from their youth, and are not always of noble birth, or liberal education. When a great office is vacant, either by death or disgrace (which often happens),

five or six of those candidates petition the Emperor to entertain his Majesty and the court with a dance on the rope, and whoever jumps the highest without falling, succeeds in the office. Very often the chief ministers themselves are commanded to show their skill, and to convince the Emperor that they have not lost their faculty. Flimnap, the Treasurer, is allowed to cut a caper on the straight rope, at least an inch higher than any other lord in the whole empire. I have seen him do the summerset several times together upon a trencher fixed on the rope, which is no thicker than a common pack-thread in England. My friend Reldresal, principal Secretary for Private Affairs, is, in my opinion, if I am not partial, the second after the Treasurer; the rest of the great officers are much upon a par.

These diversions are often attended with fatal accidents, whereof great numbers are on record. I myself have seen two or three candidates break a limb. But the danger is much greater when the ministers themselves are commanded to show their dexterity; for, by contending to excel themselves and their fellows, they strain so far, that there is hardly one of them who hath not received a fall, and some of them two or three. I was assured that a year or two before my arrival, Flimnap would have infallibly broke his neck, if one of the King's cushions, that accidentally lay on the ground, had not weakened the force of his fall.

There is likewise another diversion, which is only shown before the Emperor and Empress, and first minister, upon particular occasions. The Emperor lays on the table three fine silken threads of six inches long. One is blue, the other red, and the third green.* These threads are proposed as prizes for those persons whom the Emperor hath a mind to distinguish by a peculiar mark of his favor. The ceremony is performed in his Majesty's great chamber of state, where the candidates are to undergo a trial of dexterity very different from the former, and such as I have not observed the least resemblance of in any other country of the old or the new world. The Emperor holds a stick in his hands, both ends parallel to the horizon, while the candidates advancing one by one, sometimes leap over the stick, sometimes creep under it backward and forward several times, according as the stick is advanced or depressed. Sometimes the Emperor holds one end of the stick, and his first minister the other; sometimes the minister has it entirely to himself. Whoever performs his part with most agility, and holds out the longest in leaping and creeping, is rewarded with the blue-colored silk; the red is given to the next, and the green to the third, which they all wear girt twice round about the middle; and you see few great persons about this court, who are not adorned with one of these girdles.

The horses of the army, and those of the royal stables, having been daily led before me, were no longer shy, but would come up to my very feet without starting. The riders would leap them over my hand as I held it on the ground, and one of the Emperor's huntsmen, upon a large courser, took my foot, shoe and all; which was indeed a prodigious leap. I had the good fortune to divert the Emperor one day after a very extraordinary manner. I desired he would order several sticks of two foot high, and the thickness of an ordinary cane, to be brought me; whereupon his Majesty commanded the master of his woods to give directions accordingly; and the next morning six woodmen arrived with as many carriages, drawn by eight horses to each. I took nine of these sticks, fixing them firmly in the ground in a quadrangular figure, two foot and a half square. I took four other sticks, and tied them parallel

* Climbing, creeping, and rope-dancing are ways of winning court-favors: in England blue, red, and green ribbons represent the great orders of the Garter, the Bath, and the Thistle.

at each corner, about two foot from the ground; then I fastened my handkerchief to the nine sticks that stood erect, and extended it on all sides, till it was tight as the top of a drum; and the four parallel sticks rising about five inches higher than the handkerchief, served as ledges on each side. When I had finished my work, I desired the Emperor to let a troop of his best horse, twenty-four in number, come and exercise upon this plain. His Majesty approved of the proposal, and I took them up, one by one, in my hands, ready mounted and armed, with the proper officers to exercise them. As soon as they got into order, they divided into two parties, performed mock skirmishes, discharged blunt arrows, drew their swords, fled and pursued, attacked and retired, and in short discovered the best military discipline I ever beheld. The parallel sticks secured them and their horses from falling over the stage; and the Emperor was so much delighted, that he ordered this entertainment to be repeated several days, and once was pleased to be lifted up and give the word of command; and, with great difficulty, persuaded even the Empress herself to let me hold her in her close chair within two yards of the stage, from whence she was able to take a full view of the whole performance. It was my good fortune that no ill accident happened in these entertainments, only once a fiery horse, that belonged to one of the captains, pawing with his hoof, struck a hole in my handkerchief, and his foot slipping, he overthrew his rider and himself; but I immediately relieved them both, and covering the hole with one hand, I set down the troop with the other, in the same manner as I took them up. The horse that fell was strained in the left shoulder, but the rider got no hurt, and I repaired my handkerchief as well as I could; however, I would not trust to the strength of it any more in such dangerous enterprises.

About two or three days before I was set at liberty, as I was entertaining the court with this kind of feats, there arrived an express to inform his Majesty, that some of his subjects riding near the place where I was first taken up, had seen a great black substance lying on the ground, very oddly shaped, extending its edges round as wide as his Majesty's bedchamber, and rising up in the middle as high as a man; that it was no living creature, as they at first apprehended, for it lay on the grass without motion, and some of them had walked round it several times: that by mounting upon each other's shoulders, they had got to the top, which was flat and even, and stamping upon it they found it was hollow within; that they humbly conceived it might be something belonging to the Man-Mountain; and if his Majesty pleased, they would undertake to bring it with only five horses. I presently knew what they meant, and was glad at heart to receive this intelligence. It seems upon my first reaching the shore after our shipwreck, I was in such confusion, that before I came to the place where I went to sleep, my hat, which I had fastened with a string to my head while I was rowing, and had stuck on all the time I was swimming, fell off after I came to land; the string, as I conjecture, breaking by some accident which I never observed, but thought my hat had been lost at sea. I intreated his Imperial Majesty to give orders it might be brought to me as soon as possible, describing to him the use and the nature of it: and the next day the wagoners arrived with it, but not in a very good condition; they had bored two holes in the brim, within an inch and half of the edge, and fastened two hooks in the holes; these hooks were tied by a long cord to the harness, and thus my hat was dragged along for above half an English mile; but the ground in that country being extremely smooth and level, it received less damage than I expected.

Two days after this adventure, the Emperor, having ordered that part of his army which quarters in and about his metropolis to be in readiness, took a fancy of diverting himself in a very singular manner. He desired I would stand like a Colossus, with my legs as far asunder as I conveniently could. He then commanded his General (who was an old experienced leader, and a great patron of mine) to draw up the troops in close order, and march them under me: the foot by twenty-four in a breast, and the horse by sixteen, with drums beating, colors flying, and pikes advanced. This body consisted of three thousand foot, and a thousand horse.

I had sent so many memorials and petitions for my liberty, that his Majesty at length mentioned the matter, first in the cabinet, and then in a full council; where it was opposed by none, except Skyresh Bolgolam, who was pleased, without any provocation, to be my mortal enemy. But it was carried against him by the whole board, and confirmed by the Emperor. That minister was *Galbet,* or Admiral of the Realm, very much in his master's confidence, and a person well versed in affairs, but of a morose and sour complexion. However, he was at length persuaded to comply; but prevailed that the articles and conditions upon which I should be set free, and to which I must swear, should be drawn up by himself. These articles were brought to me by Skyresh Bolgolam in person, attended by two under-secretaries, and several persons of distinction. After they were read, I was demanded to swear to the performance of them; first in the manner of my own country, and afterwards in the method prescribed by their laws; which was to hold my right foot in my left hand, to place the middle finger of my right hand on the crown of my head, and my thumb on the tip of my right ear. But because the reader may be curious to have some idea of the style and manner of expression peculiar to that people, as well as to know the articles upon which I recovered my liberty, I have made a translation of the whole instrument word for word, as near as I was able, which I here offer to the public.

> GOLBASTO MOMAREM EVLAME GURDILO SHEFIN MULLY ULLY GUE, most mighty Emperor of Lilliput, delight and terror of the universe, whose dominions extend five thousand *blustrugs* (about twelve miles in circumference) to the extremities of the globe; monarch of all monarchs, taller than the sons of men; whose feet press down to the center, and whose head strikes against the sun; at whose nod the princes of the earth shake their knees; pleasant as the spring, comfortable as the summer, fruitful as autumn, dreadful as winter. His most sublime Majesty proposeth to the Man-Mountain, lately arrived to our celestial dominions, the following articles, which by a solemn oath he shall be obliged to perform.
>
> First, The Man-Mountain shall not depart from our dominions, without our license under our great seal.
>
> 2d, He shall not presume to come into our metropo-

lis, without our express order; at which time, the inhabitants shall have two hours warning to keep within their doors.

3d, The said Man-Mountain shall confine his walks to our principal high roads, and not offer to walk or lie down in a meadow or field of corn.

4th, As he walks the said roads, he shall take the utmost care not to trample upon the bodies of any of our loving subjects, their horses, or carriages, nor take any of our subjects into his hands, without their own consent.

5th, If an express requires extraordinary dispatch, the Man-Mountain shall be obliged to carry in his pocket the messenger and horse a six days journey once in every moon, and return the said messenger back (if so required) safe to our Imperial Presence.

6th, He shall be our ally against our enemies in the Island of Blefuscu, and do his utmost to destroy their fleet, which is now preparing to invade us.

7th, That the said Man-Mountain shall, at his times of leisure, be aiding and assisting to our workmen, in helping to raise certain great stones, toward covering the wall of the principal park, and other of our royal buildings.

8th, That the said Man-Mountain shall, in two moons' time, deliver in an exact survey of the circumference of our dominions by a computation of his own paces round the coast.

Lastly, That upon his solemn oath to observe all the above articles, the said Man-Mountain shall have a daily allowance of meat and drink sufficient for the support of 1728 of our subjects, with free access to our Royal Person, and other marks of our favor. Given at our Palace at Belfaborac the twelfth day of the ninety-first moon of our reign.

I swore and subscribed to these articles with great cheerfulness and content, although some of them were not so honorable as I could have wished; which proceeded wholly from the malice of Skyresh Bolgolam, the High-Admiral: whereupon my chains were immediately unlocked, and I was at full liberty; the Emperor himself in person did me the honor to be by at the whole ceremony. I made my acknowledgments by prostrating myself at his Majesty's feet: but he commanded me to rise; and after many gracious expressions, which, to avoid the censure of vanity, I shall not repeat, he added, that he hoped I should prove a useful servant, and well deserve all the favors he had already conferred upon me, or might do for the future.

The reader may please to observe, that in the last article for the recovery of my liberty, the Emperor stipulates to allow me a quantity of meat and drink sufficient for the support of 1728 Lilliputians. Sometime after, asking a friend at court how they came to fix on that determinate number, he told me that his Majesty's mathematicians, having taken the height of my body by the help of a quadrant, and finding it to exceed theirs in the proportion of twelve to one, they concluded from the similarity of their bodies, that mine must contain at least 1728 of theirs, and consequently would require as much food as was necessary to support that number of Lilliputians. By which, the reader may conceive an idea of the ingenuity of that people, as well as the prudent and exact economy of so great a prince.

Mildendo, *the metropolis of* Lilliput, *described, together with the Emperor's palace—A conversation between the Author and a principal Secretary, concerning the affairs of that empire—The Author's offers to serve the Emperor in his wars.*

The first request I made after I had obtained my liberty, was, that I might have license to see Mildendo, the metropolis; which the Emperor easily granted me, but with a special charge to do no hurt either to the inhabitants or their houses. The people had notice by proclamation of my design to visit the town. The wall which encompassed it, is two foot and a half high, and at least eleven inches broad, so that a coach and horses may be driven very safely round it; and it is flanked with strong towers at ten foot distance. I stepped over the great Western Gate, and passed very gently, and sidelong

through the two principal streets, only in my short waistcoat, for fear of damaging the roofs and eaves of the houses with the skirts of my coat. I walked with the utmost circumspection, to avoid treading on any stragglers, that might remain in the streets, although the orders were very strict, that all people should keep in their houses, at their own peril. The garret windows and tops of houses were so crowded with spectators, that I thought in all my travels I had not seen a more populous place. The city is an exact square, each side of the wall being five hundred foot long. The two great streets, which run across and divide it into four quarters, are five foot wide. The lanes and alleys, which I would not enter, but only viewed them as I passed, are from twelve to eighteen inches. The town is capable of holding five hundred thousand souls. The houses are from three to five stories. The shops and markets well provided.

The Emperor's palace is in the center of the city, where the two great streets meet. It is inclosed by a wall of two foot high, and twenty foot distant from the buildings. I had his Majesty's permission to step over this wall; and the space being so wide between that and the palace, I would easily view it on every side. The outward court is a square of forty foot, and includes two other courts: in the inmost are the royal apartments, which I was very desirous to see, but found it extremely difficult; for the great gates, from one square into another, were but eighteen inches high, and seven inches wide. Now the buildings of the outer court were at least five foot high, and it was impossible for me to stride over them without infinite damage to the pile, though the walls were strongly built of hewn stone, and four inches thick. At the same time the Emperor had a great desire that I should see the magnificence of his palace; but this I was not able to do till three days after, which I spent in cutting down with my knife some of the largest trees in the royal park, about a hundred yards distant from the city. Of these trees I made two stools, each about three foot high, and strong enough to bear my weight. The people having received notice a second time, I went again through the city to the palace, with my two stools in my hands. When I came to the side of the outer court, I stood upon one stool, and took the other in my hand: this I lifted over the roof, and gently set it down on the space between the first and second court, which was eight foot wide. I then stepped over the buildings very conveniently from one stool to the other, and drew up the first after me with a hooked stick. By this contrivance I got into the inmost court; and lying down upon my side, I applied my face to the windows of the middle stories, which were left open on purpose, and discovered the most splendid apartments that can be imagined. There I saw the Empress and the young Princes, in their several lodgings, with their chief attendants about them. Her Imperial Majesty was pleased to smile very graciously upon me, and gave me out of the window her hand to kiss.

But I shall not anticipate the reader with farther descriptions of this kind, because I reserve them for a greater work which is now almost ready for the press, containing a general description of this empire, from its first erection, through a long series of princes, with a particular account of their wars and politics, laws, learning, and religion: their plants and animals, their peculiar manners and customs, with other matters very curious and useful; my chief design at present being only to relate such events and transactions as happened to the public, or to myself, during a residence of about nine months in that empire.

One morning, about a fortnight after I had obtained my liberty, Reldresal, principal Secretary (as they style him) of Private Affairs, came to my house attended only by one servant. He ordered his coach to wait at a distance, and desired I would give him an hour's audience; which I readily consented to, on account of his quality and personal merits, as well as the many good offices he had done me during my solicitations at court. I offered to lie down, that he might the more conveniently reach my ear; but he chose rather to let me hold him in my hand during our conversation. He began with compliments on my liberty; said he might pretend to some merit in it: but, however, added, that if it had not been for the present situation of things at court, perhaps I might not have obtained it so soon. For, said he, as flourishing a condition as we may appear to be in to foreigners, we labor under two mighty evils; a violent faction at home, and the danger of an invasion by a most potent enemy from abroad. As to the first, you are to understand, that for about seventy moons past there have been two struggling parties in this empire, under the names of *Tramecksan* and *Slamecksan,* from the high and low heels on their shoes, by which they distinguish themselves.* It is alleged indeed, that the high heels are most agreeable to our ancient constitution: but however this be, his Majesty hath determined to make use of only low heels in the administration of the government, and all offices in the gift of the Crown, as you cannot but observe; and particularly, that his Majesty's Imperial heels are lower at least by a drurr than any of his court; (*drurr* is a measure about the fourteenth part of an inch). The animosities between these two parties run so high, that they will neither eat nor drink, nor talk with each other. We compute the *Tramecksan,* or High-Heels, to exceed us in number; but the power is wholly on our side. We apprehend his Imperial Highness, the Heir to the Crown, to have some tendency toward the High-Heels; at least we can plainly discover one of his heels higher than the other, which gives him a hobble in his gait. Now, in the midst of these intestine disquiets, we are threatened with an invasion from the Island of Blefuscu,† which is the other great empire of the universe, almost as large and powerful as this of his Majesty. For as to what we have heard

* High Heels and Low Heels: in England there were the High Church and the Low Church Parties between which there were bitter feuds.

† The Island of Blefuscu stood in relation to Lilliput as France to England.

you affirm, that there are other kingdoms and states in the world inhabited by human creatures as large as yourself, our philosophers are in much doubt, and would rather conjecture that you dropped from the moon, or one of the stars; because it is certain, that a hundred mortals of your bulk would, in a short time, destroy all the fruits and cattle of his Majesty's dominions. Besides, our histories of six thousand moons make no mention of any other regions, than the two great empires of Lilliput and Blefuscu. Which two mighty powers have, as I was going to tell you, been engaged in a most obstinate war for six and thirty moons past. It began upon the following occasion. It is allowed on all hands, that the primitive way of breaking eggs before we ate them, was upon the larger end: but his present Majesty's grandfather, while he was a boy, going to eat an egg, and breaking it according to the ancient practice, happened to cut one of his fingers. Whereupon the Emperor his father published an edict, commanding all his subjects, upon great penalties, to break the smaller end of their eggs.* The people so highly resented this law, that our histories tell us there have been six rebellions raised on that account; wherein one Emperor lost his life; and another his crown. These civil commotions were constantly fomented by the monarchs of Blefuscu; and when they were quelled, the exiles always fled for refuge to that empire. It is computed, that eleven thousand persons have, at several times, suffered death, rather than submit to break their eggs at the smaller end. Many hundred large volumes have been published upon this controversy: but the books of the Big-Endians have been long forbidden, and the whole party rendered incapable by law of holding employments. During the course of these troubles, the Emperors of Blefuscu did frequently expostulate by their ambassadors, accusing us of making a schism in religion, by offending against a fundamental doctrine of our great prophet Lustrog, in the fifty-fourth chapter of the Blundecral (which is their Alcoran). This, however, is thought to be a mere strain upon the text: for the words are these; *That all true believers break*

* The Big-Endians and the Little-Endians disputed in Lilliput as the Catholics and Protestants disputed in England in Gulliver's time.

their eggs at the convenient end: and which is the convenient end, seems, in my humble opinion, to be left to every man's conscience, or at least in the power of the chief magistrate to determine. Now the Big-Endian exiles have found so much credit in the Emperor of Blefuscu's court, and so much private assistance and encouragement from their party here at home, that a bloody war has been carried on between the two empires for six and thirty moons with various success; during which time we have lost forty capital ships, and a much greater number of smaller vessels, together with thirty thousand of our best seamen and soldiers; and the damage received by the enemy is reckoned to be somewhat greater than ours. However, they have now equipped a numerous fleet, and are just preparing to make a descent upon us; and his Imperial Majesty, placing great confidence in your valor and strength, has commanded me to lay this account of his affairs before you.

I desired the Secretary to present my humble duty to the Emperor, and to let him know, that I thought it would not become me, who was a foreigner, to interfere with parties; but I was ready, with the hazard of my life, to defend his person and state against all invaders.

The Author, by an extraordinary stratagem, prevents an invasion—A high title of honor is conferred upon him—Ambassadors arrive from the Emperor of Blefuscu, *and sue for peace.*

The Empire of Blefuscu is an island situated to the north northeast side of Lilliput, from whence it is parted only by a channel of eight hundred yards wide. I had not yet seen it, and upon this notice of an intended invasion, I avoided appearing on that side of the coast, for fear of being discovered by some of the enemy's ships, who had received no intelligence of me, all intercourse between the two empires having been strictly forbidden during the war, upon pain of death, and an embargo laid by our Emperor upon all vessels whatsoever. I communicated to his Majesty a project I had formed of seizing the enemy's whole fleet: which, as our scouts assured us, lay at anchor in the harbor ready to sail with the first fair wind. I

consulted the most experienced seamen, upon the depth of the channel, which they had often plumbed, who told me, that in the middle at high-water it was seventy *glumgluffs* deep, which is about six foot of European measure; and the rest of it fifty *glumgluffs* at most. I walked toward the northeast coast over against Blefuscu; and lying down behind a hillock, took out my small pocket perspective-glass, and viewed the enemy's fleet at anchor, consisting of about fifty men of war, and a great number of transports; I then came back to my house, and gave order (for which I had a warrant) for a great quantity of the strongest cable and bars of iron. The cable was about as thick as packthread, and the bars of the length and size of a knitting-needle. I trebled the cable to make it stronger, and for the same reason I twisted three of the iron bars together, binding the extremities into a hook. Having thus fixed fifty hooks to as many cables, I went back to the northeast coast, and putting off my coat, shoes, and stockings, walked into the sea in my leathern jerkin, about half an hour before high water. I waded with what haste I could, and swam in the middle about thirty yards till I felt ground; I arrived at the fleet in less than half an hour. The enemy was so frightened when they saw me, that they leaped out of their ships, and swam to shore, where there could not be fewer than thirty thousand souls. I then took my tackling, and fastening a hook to the hole at the prow of each, I tied all the cords together at the end. While I was thus employed, the enemy discharged several thousand arrows, many of which stuck in my hands and face; and besides the excessive smart, gave me much disturbance in my work. My greatest apprehension was for my eyes, which I should have infallibly lost, if I had not suddenly thought of an expedient. I kept among other little necessaries a pair of spectacles in a private pocket, which, as I observed before, had escaped the Emperor's searchers. These I took out and fastened as strongly as I could upon my nose, and thus armed went on boldly with my work in spite of the enemy's arrows, many of which struck against the glasses of my spectacles, but without any other effect, further than a little to discompose them. I had now fastened all the hooks, and taking the knot in my hand, began to pull; but not a ship would stir, for they were all too fast held by their anchors, so that the boldest part of my enterprise remained. I therefore let go the cord, and leaving the hooks fixed to the ships, I resolutely cut with my knife the cables that fastened the anchors, receiving about two hundred shots in my face and hands; then I took up the knotted end of the cables, to which my hooks were tied, and with great ease drew fifty of the enemy's largest men of war after me.*

The Blefuscudians, who had not the least imagination of what I intended, were at first confounded with astonishment. They had seen me cut the cables, and thought my design was only to let the ships run adrift, or fall foul on each other: but when they perceived the whole fleet moving in order, and saw me pulling at the end, they set up such a scream of grief and despair, that it is almost impossible to describe or conceive. When I had got out of danger, I stopped awhile to pick out the arrows that stuck in my hands and face; and rubbed on some of the same ointment that was given me at my first arrival, as I have formerly mentioned. I then took off my spectacles, and waiting about an hour, till the tide was a little fallen, I waded through the middle with my cargo, and arrived safe at the royal port of Lilliput.

The Emperor and his whole court stood on the shore, expecting the issue of this great adventure. They saw the ships move forward in a large half-moon, but could not discern me,

* Mathematicians doubt if Gulliver could have done this. It would be the same as dragging a boat that would hold seventeen or eighteen men. Could a man up to his neck in water do this, they ask?

who was up to my breast in water. When I advanced to the middle of the channel, they were yet in more pain, because I was under water to my neck. The Emperor concluded me to be drowned, and that the enemy's fleet was approaching in a hostile manner: but he was soon eased of his fears, for the channel growing shallower every step I made, I came in a short time within hearing, and holding up the end of the cable by which the fleet was fastened, I cried in a loud voice, *Long live the most puissant Emperor of Lilliput!* This great prince received me at my landing with all possible encomiums, and created me a *Nardac* upon the spot, which is the highest title of honor among them.

His Majesty desired I would take some other opportunity of bringing all the rest of his enemy's ships into his ports. And so unmeasurable is the ambition of princes, that he seemed to think of nothing less than reducing the whole empire of Blefuscu into a province, and governing it by a viceroy; of destroying the Big-Endian exiles, and compelling that people to break the smaller end of their eggs, by which he would remain the sole monarch of the whole world. But I endeavored to divert him from this design, by many arguments drawn from the topics of policy as well as justice; and I plainly protested, that I would never be an instrument of bringing a free and brave people into slavery. And when the matter was debated in council, the wisest part of the ministry were of my opinion.

This open bold declaration of mine was so opposite to the schemes and politics of his Imperial Majesty, that he could never forgive it; he mentioned it in a very artful manner at council, where I was told that some of the wisest appeared, at least by their silence, to be of my opinion; but others, who were my secret enemies, could not forbear some expressions, which by a side-wind reflected on me. And from this time began an intrigue between his Majesty and a junto of ministers maliciously bent against me, which broke out in less than two months, and had like to have ended in my utter destruction. Of so little weight are the greatest services to princes, when put into the balance with a refusal to gratify their passions.

About three weeks after this exploit, there arrived a solemn embassy from Blefuscu, with humble offers of a peace; which was soon concluded upon conditions very advantageous to our Emperor, wherewith I shall not trouble the reader. There were six ambassadors, with a train of about five hundred persons, and their entry was very magnificent, suitable to the grandeur of their master, and the importance of their business. When their treaty was finished, wherein I did them several good offices by the credit I now had, or at least appeared to have at court, their Excellencies, who were privately told how much I had been their friend, made me a visit in form. They began with many compliments upon my valor and generosity, invited me to that kingdom in the Emperor their master's name, and desired me to show them some proofs of my prodigious strength, of which they had heard so many wonders; wherein I readily obliged them, but shall not trouble the reader with the particulars.

When I had for some time entertained their Excellencies, to their infinite satisfaction and surprise, I desired they would do me the honor to present my most humble respects to the Emperor their master, the renown of whose virtues had so justly filled the whole world with admiration, and whose royal person I resolved to attend before I returned to my own country: accordingly, the next time I had the honor to see our Emperor, I desired his general license to wait on the Blefuscudian monarch, which he was pleased to grant me, as I could perceive, in a very cold manner; but could not guess the reason, till I had a whisper from a certain person, that Flimnap and Bolgolam had represented my intercourse with those ambassadors as a mark of disaffection, from which I am sure my heart was wholly free. And this was the first time I began to conceive some imperfect idea of courts and ministers.

It is to be observed, that these ambassadors spoke to me by an interpreter, the languages of both empires differing as much from each other as any two in Europe, and each nation priding itself upon the antiquity, beauty, and energy of their own tongues, with an avowed contempt for that of their neighbor; yet our Emperor, standing upon the advantage he had got by the seizure of their fleet, obliged them to deliver their credentials, and make their speech in the Lilliputian tongue. And it must be confessed, that from the great intercourse of trade and commerce between both realms, from the continual reception of exiles, which is mutual among them, and from the custom in each empire to send their young nobility and richer gentry to the other, in order to polish themselves by seeing the world, and understanding men and manners; there are few persons of distinction, or merchants, or seamen, who dwell in the maritime parts, but what can hold conversation in both tongues; as I found some weeks after, when I went to pay my respects to the Emperor of Blefuscu, which in the midst of great misfortunes, through the malice of my enemies, proved a very happy adventure to me, as I shall relate in its proper place.

Of the inhabitants of Lilliput; *their learning, laws, and customs, the manner of educating their children—The Author's way of living in that country—His vindication of a great lady.*

Although I intend to leave the description of this empire to a particular treatise, yet in the meantime I am content to gratify the curious reader with some general ideas. As the common size of the natives is somewhat under six inches high, so there is an exact proportion in all other animals, as well as plants and trees: for instance, the tallest horses and oxen are between four and five inches in height, the sheep an inch and a half, more or less: their geese about the bigness of a sparrow, and so the several gradations downward till you come to the smallest, which, to my sight, were almost invisible; but nature hath adapted the eyes of the Lilliputians to all objects proper for their view: they see with great exactness, but at no great distance. And to show the sharpness of their sight toward objects that are near, I have been much pleased with observing a cook pulling a lark, which was not so large as a common fly; and a young girl threading an invisible needle with invisible silk. Their tallest trees are about seven foot high: I mean some of those in the great royal park, the tops whereof I could but just reach with my fist clinched. The other vegetables are in the same proportion; but this I leave to the reader's imagination.

I shall say but little at present of their learning, which for many ages hath flourished in all its branches among them: but

their manner of writing is very peculiar, being neither from the left to the right, like the Europeans; nor from the right to the left, like the Arabians; nor from up to down, like the Chinese; nor from down to up, like the Cascagians; but aslant from one corner of the paper to the other, like ladies in England.

They bury their dead with their heads directly downward, because they hold an opinion, that in eleven thousand moons they are all to rise again, in which period the earth (which they conceive to be flat) will turn upside down, and by this means they shall, at their resurrection, be found ready standing on their feet. The learned among them confess the absurdity of this doctrine, but the practice still continues, in compliance to the vulgar.

There are some laws and customs in this empire very peculiar; and if they were not so directly contrary to those of my own dear country, I should be tempted to say a little in their justification. It is only to be wished, that they were as well executed. The first I shall mention, relates to informers. All crimes against the state are punished here with the utmost severity; but if the person accused maketh his innocence plainly to appear upon his trial, the accuser is immediately put to an ignominious death; and out of his goods or lands, the innocent person is quadruply recompensed for the loss of his time, for the danger he underwent, for the hardship of his imprisonment, and for all the charges he hath been at in making his defense. Or, if that fund be deficient, it is largely supplied by the Crown. The Emperor does also confer on him some public mark of his favor, and proclamation is made of his innocence through the whole city.

They look upon fraud as a greater crime than theft, and therefore seldom fail to punish it with death; for they allege, that care and vigilance, with a very common understanding, may preserve a man's goods from thieves, but honesty has no fence against superior cunning; and since it is necessary that there should be a perpetual intercourse of buying and selling, and dealing upon credit, where fraud is permitted and connived at, or hath no law to punish it, the honest dealer is always undone, and the knave gets the advantage. I remember when I was once interceding with the Emperor for a criminal who had wronged his master of a great sum of money, which he had received by order, and ran away with; and happening to tell his Majesty, by way of extenuation, that it was only a breach of trust; the Emperor thought it monstrous in me to offer, as a defense, the greatest aggravation of the crime: and truly I had little to say in return, farther than the common answer, that different nations had different customs; for, I confess, I was heartily ashamed.

Although we usually call reward and punishment the two hinges upon which all government turns, yet I could never observe this maxim to be put in practice by any nation except that of Lilliput. Whoever can there bring sufficient proof that he hath strictly observed the laws of his country for seventy-three moons, hath a claim to certain privileges, according to his quality and condition of life, with a proportionable sum of money out of a fund appropriated for that use: he likewise acquires the title of *Snilpall*, or Legal, which is added to his name, but does not descend to his posterity. And these people thought it a prodigious defect of policy among us, when I told them that our laws were enforced only by penalties, without any mention of reward. It is upon this account that the image of Justice, in their courts of judicature, is formed with six eyes, two before, as many behind, and on each side one, to signify circumspection; with a bag of gold open in her right hand, and a sword sheathed in her left, to show she is more disposed to reward than to punish.

It may perhaps divert the curious reader, to give some account of my domestic, and my manner of living in this country, during a residence of nine months and thirteen days. Having a head mechanically turned, and being likewise forced by necessity, I had made for myself a table and chair convenient enough, out of the largest trees in the royal park. Two hundred sempstresses were employed to make me shirts, and linen for my bed and table, all of the strongest and coarsest kind they could get; which, however, they were forced to quilt together in several folds, for the thickest was some degrees finer than lawn. Their linen is usually three inches wide, and three foot make a piece. The sempstresses took my measure as I lay on the ground, one standing at my neck, and another at my mid-leg, with a strong cord extended, that each held by the end, while the third measured the length of the cord with a rule of an inch long. Then they measured my right thumb, and desired no more; for by a mathematical computation, that twice round the thumb is once round the wrist, and so on to the neck and the waist, and by the help of my old shirt, which I displayed on the ground before them for a pattern, they fitted me exactly. Three hundred tailors were employed in the same manner to make me clothes; but they had another contrivance for taking my measure. I kneeled down, and they raised a ladder from the ground to my neck; upon this ladder one of them mounted, and let fall a plumb-line from my collar to the floor, which just answered the length of my coat: but my waist and arms I measured myself. When my clothes were finished, which was done in my house (for the largest of theirs would not have been able to hold them), they looked like the patch-work made by the ladies in England, only that mine were all of a color.

I had three hundred cooks to dress my victuals, in little convenient huts built about my house, where they and their families lived, and prepared me two dishes apiece. I took up twenty waiters in my hand, and placed them on the table: a hundred more attended below on the ground, some with dishes of meat, and some with barrels of wine, and other liquors, slung on their shoulders; all which the waiters above drew up as I wanted, in a very ingenious manner, by certain cords, as we draw the bucket up a well in Europe. A dish of their meat was a good mouthful, and a barrel of their liquor a reasonable draught. Their mutton yields to ours, but their beef is excellent. I have had a sirloin so large, that I have been forced to make three bits of it; but this is rare. My servants were astonished to see me eat it bones and all, as in our country we do the leg of a lark. Their geese and turkeys I usually ate at a mouthful, and I must confess they far exceed ours. Of their smaller fowl I could take up twenty or thirty at the end of my knife.

One day his Imperial Majesty, being informed of my way of living, desired that himself and his Royal Consort, with the young Princes of the blood of both sexes, might have the happiness (as he was pleased to call it) of dining with me. They came accordingly, and I placed them in chairs of state on my table, just over against me, with their guards about them. Flimnap, the Lord High Treasurer, attended there likewise with his white staff; and I observed he often looked on me with a sour countenance, which I would not seem to regard, but ate more than usual, in honor to my dear country, as well as to fill the court with admiration. I have some private reasons to believe, that this visit from his Majesty gave Flimnap an opportunity of doing me ill offices to his master. That minister had always been my secret enemy, though he outwardly caressed me more than was usual to the moroseness of his nature. He represented to the Emperor the low condition of his treasury; that he was forced to take up money at great discount; that exchequer bills would not circulate under nine per cent below par; that in short I had cost his Majesty above a million and half of *sprugs* (their greatest gold coin, about the bigness of a spangle); and upon the whole, that it would be advisable in the Emperor to take the first fair occasion of dismissing me.

I am here obliged to vindicate the reputation of an excellent lady, who was an innocent sufferer upon my account. The Treasurer took a fancy to be jealous of his wife, from the malice of some evil tongues, who informed him that her Grace had taken a violent affection for my person; and the court-scandal ran for some time, that she once came privately to my lodging. This I solemnly declare to be a most infamous falsehood, without any grounds, farther than that her Grace was pleased to treat me with all innocent marks of freedom and friendship. I own she came often to my house, but always publicly, nor even without three more in the coach, who were usually her sister and young daughter, and some particular acquaintance; but this was common to many other ladies of the court. And I still appeal to my servants round, whether they at any time saw a coach at my door without knowing what persons were in it. On those occasions, when a servant had given me notice, my custom was to go immediately to the door; and, after paying my respects, to take up the coach and two horses very carefully in my hands (for, if there were six horses, the postilion always unharnessed four) and place them on a table, where I had fixed a movable rim quite round, of five inches high, to prevent accidents. And I have often had four coaches and horses at once on my table full of company, while I sat in my chair leaning my face toward them; and when I was engaged with one set, the coachmen would gently drive the others round my table. I have passed many an afternoon very agreeably in these conversations. But I defy the Treasurer, or his two informers (I will name them, and let them make their best of it) Clustril and Drunlo, to prove that any person ever came to me *incognito*, except the secretary Reldresal, who was sent by express command of his Imperial Majesty, as I have before related. I should not have dwelt so long upon this particular, if it had not been a point wherein the reputation of a great lady is so nearly concerned, to say nothing of my own; though I then had the honor to be a *Nardac*, which the Treasurer himself is not; for all the world knows he is only a *Glumglum*, a title inferior by one degree, as that of a Marquis is to a Duke in England, although I allow he preceded me in right of his post. These false informations, which I afterwards came to the knowledge of, by an accident not proper to mention, made Flimnap, the Treasurer, show his lady for some time an ill countenance, and me a worse; and although he were at last undeceived and reconciled to her, yet I lost all credit with him, and found my interest decline very fast with the Emperor himself, who was indeed too much governed by that favorite.

The Author, being informed of a design to accuse him of high treason, makes his escape to Blefuscu—*His reception there.*

Before I proceed to give an account of my leaving this kingdom, it may be proper to inform the reader of a private intrigue which had been for two months forming against me.

I had been hitherto all my life a stranger to courts, for which I was unqualified by the meanness of my condition. I had indeed heard and read enough of the dispositions of great princes and ministers; but never expected to have found such terrible effects of them in so remote a country, governed, as I thought, by very different maxims from those in Europe.

When I was just preparing to pay my attendance on the Emperor of Blefuscu, a considerable person at court (to whom I had been very serviceable at a time when he lay under the highest displeasure of his Imperial Majesty) came to my house very privately at night in a close chair, and without sending his name, desired admittance. The chairmen were dismissed; I put the chair, with his Lordship in it, into my coat-pocket: and giving orders to a trusty servant to say I was indisposed and gone to sleep, I fastened the door of my house, placed the chair on the table, according to my usual custom, and sat down by it. After the common salutations were over, observing his Lordship's countenance full of concern, and inquiring into the reason, he desired I would hear him with patience in a matter that highly concerned my honor and my life. His speech was to the following effect, for I took notes of it as soon as he left me.

"You are to know," said he, "that several Committees of Council have been lately called in the most private manner on your account; and it is but two days since his Majesty came to a full resolution.

"You are very sensible that Skyresh Bolgolam (*Galbet,* or High Admiral) hath been your mortal enemy almost ever since your arrival. His original reasons I know not; but his hatred is much increased since your great success against Blefuscu, by which his glory, as Admiral, is obscured. This Lord, in conjunction with Flimnap the High Treasurer, whose enmity against you is notorious on account of his lady, Limtoc the

General, Lalcon the Chamberlain, and Balmuff the Grand Justiciary, have prepared articles of impeachment against you, for treason, and other capital crimes."

This preface made me so impatient, being conscious of my own merits and innocence, that I was going to interrupt; when he entreated me to be silent, and thus proceeded.

"Out of gratitude for the favors you have done me, I procured information of the whole proceedings, and a copy of the articles, wherein I venture my head for your service."

Articles of Impeachment against Quinbus Flestrin (*the* Man-Mountain).

That the said Quinbus Flestrin having brought the imperial fleet of Blefuscu into the royal port, and being afterwards commanded by his Imperial Majesty to seize all the other ships of the said empire of Blefuscu, and reduce that empire to a province, to be governed by a viceroy from hence, and to destroy and put to death not only all the Big-Endian exiles, but likewise all the people of that empire, who would not immediately forsake the Big-Endian heresy: He, the said Flestrin, like a false traitor against his most Auspicious, Serene, Imperial Majesty, did petition to be excused from the said service, upon pretense of unwillingness to force the consciences, or destroy the liberties and lives of an innocent people.

* * *

That, whereas certain ambassadors arrived from the

> court of Blefuscu, to sue for peace in his Majesty's court: He, the said Flestrin, did, like a false traitor, aid, abet, comfort, and divert the said ambassadors, although he knew them to be servants to a Prince who was lately an open enemy to his Imperial Majesty, and in open war against his said Majesty.
>
> * * *
>
> That the said Quinbus Flestrin, contrary to the duty of a faithful subject, is now preparing to make a voyage to the court and empire of Blefuscu, for which he hath received only verbal license from his Imperial Majesty; and under color of the said license, doth falsely and traitorously intend to take the said voyage, and thereby to aid, comfort, and abet the Emperor of Blefuscu, so late an enemy, and in open war with his Imperial Majesty aforesaid.
>
> * * *

"There are some other articles, but these are the most important, of which I have read you an abstract.

"In the several debates upon this impeachment, it must be confessed that his Majesty gave many marks of his great lenity, often urging the services you had done him, and endeavoring to extenuate your crimes. The Treasurer and Admiral insisted that you should be put to the most painful and ignominious death, by setting fire on your house at night, and the General was to attend with twenty thousand men armed with poisoned arrows to shoot you on the face and hands. Some of your servants were to have private orders to strew a poisonous juice on your shirts, which would soon make you tear your own flesh, and die in the utmost torture. The General came into the same opinion; so that for a long time there was a majority against you. But his Majesty resolving, if possible, to spare your life, at last brought off the Chamberlain.

"Upon this incident, Reldresal, principal Secretary for Private Affairs, who always approved himself your true friend, was commanded by the Emperor to deliver his opinion, which he accordingly did; and therein justified the good thoughts you have of him. He allowed your crimes to be great, but that still there was room for mercy, the most commendable virtue in a prince, and for which his Majesty was so justly celebrated. He said, the friendship between you and him was so well known to the world, that perhaps the most honorable board might think him partial: however, in obedience to the command he had received, he would freely offer his sentiments. That if his Majesty, in consideration of your services, and pursuant to his own merciful disposition, would please to spare your life, and only gave orders to put out both your eyes, he humbly conceived, that by this expedient, justice might in some measure be satisfied, and all the world would applaud the lenity of the Emperor, as well as the fair and generous proceedings of those who have the honor to be his counselors. That the loss of your eyes would be no impediment to your bodily strength, by which you might still be useful to his Majesty. That blindness is an addition to courage, by concealing dangers from us; that the fear you had for your eyes, was the greatest difficulty in bringing over the enemy's fleet, and it would be sufficient for you to see by the eyes of the ministers, since the greatest princes do no more.

"This proposal was received with the utmost disapprobation by the whole board. Bolgolam, the Admiral, could not preserve his temper; but rising up in fury, said, he wondered how the Secretary durst presume to give his opinion for preserving the life of a traitor: that the services you had performed, were, by all true reasons of state, the great aggravation of your crimes; that the same strength which enabled you to bring over the enemy's fleet, might serve, upon the first discontent, to carry it back: that he had good reasons to think you were a Big-Endian in your heart; and as treason begins in the heart, before it appears in overt acts, so he accused you as a traitor on that account, and therefore insisted you should be put to death.

"The Treasurer was of the same opinion; he showed to what straits his Majesty's revenue was reduced by the charge of maintaining you, which would soon grow insupportable: that the Secretary's expedient of putting out your eyes was so far from being a remedy against this evil, that it would probably increase it, as it is manifest from the common practice of blinding some kind of fowl, after which they fed the faster, and grew sooner fat: that his sacred Majesty and the Council, who are your judges, were in their own consciences fully convinced of your guilt, which was a sufficient argument to condemn you to death, without the formal proofs required by the strict letter of the law.

"But his Imperial Majesty, fully determined against capital punishment, was graciously pleased to say, that since the Council thought the loss of your eyes too easy a censure, some other may be inflicted hereafter. And your friend the Secretary humbly desiring to be heard again, in answer to what the Treasurer had objected concerning the great charge his Majesty was at in maintaining you, said, that his Excellency, who had the sole disposal of the Emperor's revenue, might easily provide against that evil, by gradually lessening your establishment; by which, for want of sufficient food, you would grow weak and faint, and lose your appetite, and consequently decay and consume in a few months; and immediately upon your death, five or six thousand of his Majesty's subjects might, in two or three days, cut your flesh from your bones, take it away by cart-loads, and bury it in distant parts to prevent infection, leaving the skeleton as a monument of admiration to posterity.

"Thus by the great friendship of the Secretary, the whole affair was compromised. It was strictly enjoined, that the project of starving you by degrees should be kept a secret, but the sentence of putting out your eyes was entered on the books; none dissenting except Bolgolam the Admiral.

"In three days your friend the Secretary will be directed to come to your house, and read before you the articles of impeachment; and then to signify the great lenity and favor of his Majesty and Council, whereby you are only condemned to the loss of your eyes, which his Majesty doth not question you will gratefully and humbly submit to; and twenty of his Majesty's surgeons will attend, in order to see the operation well performed, by discharging very sharp-pointed arrows into the balls of your eyes, as you lie on the ground.

"I leave to your prudence what measures you will take; and to avoid suspicion, I must immediately return in as private a manner as I came."

His Lordship did so, and I remained alone, under many doubts and perplexities of mind.

It was a custom introduced by this prince and his ministry (very different, as I have been assured, from the practices of former times), that after the court had decreed any cruel execution, either to gratify the monarch's resentment, or the malice of a favorite, the Emperor always made a speech to his whole Council, expressing his great lenity and tenderness, as qualities known and confessed by all the world. This speech was immediately published through the kingdom; nor did anything terrify the people so much as those encomiums on his Majesty's mercy; because it was observed, that the more these praises were enlarged and insisted on, the more inhuman was the punishment, and the sufferer more innocent. And as to myself, I must confess, having never been designed for a courtier either by my birth or education, I was so ill a judge of things, that I could not discover the lenity and favor of this sentence, but conceived it (perhaps erroneously) rather to be rigorous than gentle. I sometimes thought of standing my trial, for although I could not deny the facts alleged in the several articles, yet I hoped they would admit of some extenuations. But having in my life perused many state trials, which I ever observed to terminate as the judges thought fit to direct, I durst not rely on so dangerous a decision, in so critical a juncture, and against such powerful enemies. Once I was strongly bent upon resistance, for while I had liberty, the whole strength of that empire could hardly subdue me, and I might easily with stones pelt the metropolis to pieces; but I soon rejected that project with horror, by remembering the oath I had made to the Emperor, the favors I received from him, and the high title of *Nardac* he conferred upon me. Neither had I so soon learned the gratitude of courtiers, to persuade myself that his Majesty's present severities acquitted me of all past obligations.

At last I fixed upon a resolution, for which it is probable I may incur some censure, and not unjustly; for I confess I owe the preserving of my eyes, and consequently my liberty, to my own great rashness and want of experience: because if I had then known the nature of princes and ministers, which I have since observed in many other courts, and their methods of treating criminals less obnoxious than myself, I should with great alacrity and readiness have submitted to so easy a punishment. But hurried on by the precipitancy of youth, and having his Imperial Majesty's license to pay my attendance upon the Emperor of Blefuscu, I took this opportunity, before the three days were elapsed, to send a letter to my friend the Secretary, signifying my resolution of setting out that morning for Blefuscu pursuant to the leave I had got; and without waiting for an answer, I went to that side of the island where our fleet lay. I seized a large man of war, tied a cable to the prow, and, lifting up the anchors, I stripped myself, put my clothes (together with my coverlet, which I brought under my arm) into the vessel, and drawing it after me between wading and swimming, arrived at the royal port of Blefuscu, where the people had long expected me: they lent me two guides to direct me to the capital city, which is of the same name. I held them in my hands till I came within two hundred yards of a gate, and desired them to signify my arrival to one of the secretaries, and let him know, I there waited his Majesty's command. I had an answer in about an hour, that his Majesty, attended by the Royal Family, and great officers of the court, was coming out to receive me. I advanced a hundred yards. The Emperor and his train alighted from their horses, the Empress and ladies from their coaches, and I did not perceive they were in any fright or concern. I lay on the ground to kiss his Majesty's and the Empress's hands. I told his Majesty, that I was come according to my promise, and with the license of the Emperor my master, to have the honor of seeing so mighty a monarch, and to offer him any service in my power, consistent with my duty to my own prince; not mentioning a word of my disgrace, because I had hitherto no regular information of it, and might suppose myself wholly ignorant of any such design; neither could I reasonably conceive that the Emperor would discover the secret while I was out of his power: wherein, however, it soon appeared I was deceived.

I shall not trouble the reader with the particular account of my reception at this court, which was suitable to the generosity of so great a prince; nor of the difficulties I was in for want of a house and bed, being forced to lie on the ground, wrapped up in my coverlet.

The Author, by a lucky accident, finds means to leave Blefuscu; *and, after some difficulties, returns safe to his native country.*

Three days after my arrival, walking out of curiosity to the northeast coast of the island, I observed, about half a league off, in the sea, somewhat that looked like a boat overturned. I pulled off my shoes and stockings, and wading two or three hundred yards, I found the object to approach nearer by force of the tide; and then plainly saw it to be a real boat, which I supposed might, by some tempest, have been driven from a ship; whereupon I returned immediately toward the city, and desired his Imperial Majesty to lend me twenty of the tallest vessels he had left after the loss of his fleet, and three thousand seamen under the command of his Vice-Admiral. This fleet sailed round, while I went back the shortest way to the coast where I first discovered the boat; I found the tide had driven it still nearer. The seamen were all provided with cordage, which I had beforehand twisted to a sufficient strength. When the ships came up, I stripped myself, and waded till I came within an hundred yards of the boat, after which I was forced to swim till I got up to it. The seamen threw me the end of the cord, which I fastened to a hole in the forepart of the boat, and the other end to a man of war; but I found all my labor to little purpose; for being out of my depth, I was not able to work. In this necessity, I was forced to swim behind, and push the boat forward as often as I could, with one of my hands; and the tide favoring me, I advanced so far, that I could just hold up my chin and feel the ground. I rested two or three minutes, and then gave the boat another shove, and so on till the sea was no higher than my armpits; and now the most laborious part being over, I took out my other cables, which were stowed in one of the ships, and fastening them first to the boat, and then to nine of the vessels which attended me, the wind being favorable, the seamen towed, and I shoved till we arrived within forty yards of the shore; and waiting till the tide was out, I got dry to the boat, and by the assistance of two thousand men. with ropes and engines, I made a shift to turn it on its bottom and found it was but little damaged.

I shall not trouble the reader with the difficulties I was under

by the help of certain paddles, which cost me ten days making, to get my boat to the royal port of Blefuscu, where a mighty concourse of people appeared upon my arrival, full of wonder at the sight of so prodigious a vessel. I told the Emperor that my good fortune had thrown this boat in my way, to carry me to some place from whence I might return into my native country, and begged his Majesty's orders for getting materials to fit it up, together with his license to depart, which, after some kind expostulations, he was pleased to grant.

I did very much wonder, in all this time, not to have heard of any express relating to me from our Emperor to the court of Blefuscu. But I was afterwards given privately to understand, that his Imperial Majesty, never imagining I had the least notice of his designs, believed I was only gone to Blefuscu in performance of my promise, according to the license he had given me, which was well known at our court, and would return in a few days when that ceremony was ended. But he was at last in pain at my long absence; and after consulting with the Treasurer, and the rest of that cabal, a person of quality was dispatched with the copy of the articles against me. This envoy had instructions to represent to the monarch of Blefuscu, the great lenity of his master, who was content to punish me no farther than with the loss of my eyes; that I had fled from justice, and if I did not return in two hours, I should be deprived of my title of *Nardac,* and declared a traitor. The envoy further added, that in order to maintain the peace and amity between both empires, his master expected, that his brother of Blefuscu would give orders to have me sent back to Lilliput, bound hand and foot, to be punished as a traitor.

The Emperor of Blefuscu having taken three days to consult, returned an answer consisting of many civilities and excuses. He said, that as for sending me bound, his brother knew it was impossible; that although I had deprived him of his fleet, yet he owed great obligations to me for many good offices I had done him in making the peace. That, however, both their Majesties would soon be made easy; for I had found a prodigious vessel on the shore, able to carry me on the sea, which he had given order to fit up with my own assistance and direction; and he hoped in a few weeks both empires would be freed from so insupportable an incumbrance.

With this answer the envoy returned to Lilliput, and the monarch of Blefuscu related to me all that had passed; offering me at the same time (but under the strictest confidence) his gracious protection, if I would continue in his service; wherein although I believed him sincere, yet I resolved never more to put any confidence in princes or ministers, where I could possibly avoid it; and therefore, with all due acknowledgments for his favorable intentions, I humbly begged to be excused. I told him, that since fortune, whether good or evil, had thrown a vessel in my way, I was resolved to venture myself in the ocean, rather than be an occasion of difference between two such mighty monarchs. Neither did I find the Emperor at all displeased; and I discovered by a certain accident, that he was very glad of my resolution, and so were most of his ministers.

These considerations moved me to hasten my departure somewhat sooner than I intended; to which the court, impatient to have me gone, very readily contributed. Five hundred workmen were employed to make two sails to my boat, according to my directions, by quilting thirteen fold of their strongest linen together. I was at the pains of making ropes and cables, by twisting ten, twenty or thirty of the thickest and strongest of theirs. A great stone that I happened to find, after a long search, by the seashore, served me for an anchor. I had the tallow of three hundred cows for greasing my boat, and other uses. I was at incredible pains in cutting down some of the largest timber-trees for oars and masts, wherein I was, however, much assisted by his Majesty's ship carpenters, who helped me in smoothing them, after I had done the rough work.

In about a month, when all was prepared, I sent to receive his Majesty's commands, and to take my leave. The Emperor and Royal Family came out of the palace; I lay down on my face to kiss his hand, which he very graciously gave me: so did the Empress and young Princes of the blood. His Majesty presented me with fifty purses of two hundred *sprugs* apiece, together with his picture at full length, which I put immediately into one of my gloves, to keep it from being hurt. The ceremonies at my departure were too many to trouble the reader with at this time.

I stored the boat with the carcasses of an hundred oxen, and three hundred sheep, with bread and drink proportionable, and as much meat ready dressed as four hundred cooks could provide. I took with me six cows and two bulls alive, with as many ewes and rams, intending to carry them into my own country, and propagate the breed. And to feed them on board, I had a good bundle of hay, and a bag of corn. I would gladly have taken a dozen of the natives, but this was a thing the Emperor would by no means permit; and besides a diligent search into my pockets, his Majesty engaged my honor not to carry away any of his subjects, although with their own consent and desire.

Having thus prepared all things as well as I was able, I set sail on the twenty-fourth day of September, 1701, at six in the morning; and when I had gone about four leagues to the northward, the wind being at southeast, at six in the evening I descried a small island about half a league to the northwest. I advanced forward, and cast anchor on the lee-side of the island, which seemed to be uninhabited. I then took some refreshment, and went to my rest. I slept well, and as I conjecture at least six hours, for I found the day broke in two hours after I awaked. It was a clear night. I ate my breakfast before the sun was up; and heaving anchor, the wind being favorable, I steered the same course that I had done the day before, wherein I was directed by my pocket-compass. My intention was to reach, if possible, one of those islands, which I had reason to believe lay to the northeast of Van Diemen's Land. I discovered nothing all that day; but upon the next, about three in the afternoon, when I had by my computation made twenty-four leagues from Blefuscu, I descried a sail steering to the southeast; my course was due east. I hailed her, but could get no answer; yet I found I gained upon her, for the wind slackened. I made all the sail I could, and in half an hour she spied me, then hung out her ancient, and discharged a gun. It is not easy to express the joy I was in upon the unexpected hope of once more seeing my beloved country, and the dear pledges I had left in it. The ship slackened her sails, and I came up with her between five and six in the evening, September 26; but my heart leaped within me to see her English colors. I put my cows and sheep into my coat-pockets, and got on board with all my little cargo of provisions. The vessel was an English merchant-man, returning from Japan by the North and South Seas; the Captain, Mr. John Biddel of Deptford, a very civil man, and an excellent sailor. We were now in the latitude of 30 degrees south; there were about fifty men in the ship; and here I met an old comrade of mine, one Peter Williams, who gave me a good character to the Captain. This gentleman treated me with kindness, and desired I would let him know what place I came from last, and whither I was bound; which I did in a few words, but he thought I was raving, and that the dangers I underwent had disturbed my head; whereupon I took my black cattle and sheep out of my pocket, which, after great astonishment, clearly convinced him of my veracity. I then showed him the gold given me by the Emperor of Blefuscu, together with his Majesty's picture at full length, and some other rarities of that country. I gave him two purses of two hundred *sprugs* each, and promised, when we arrived in England, to make him a present of a cow and a sheep.

I shall not trouble the reader with a particular account of this voyage, which was very prosperous for the most part. We arrived in the Downs on the 13th of April, 1702. I had only one misfortune, that the rats on board carried away one of my sheep; I found her bones in a hole, picked clean from the flesh. The rest of my cattle I got safe on shore, and set them a-grazing in a bowling-green at Greenwich, where the fineness of the grass made them feed very heartily, though I had always feared the contrary: neither could I possibly have preserved them in so long a voyage, if the Captain had not allowed me some of his best biscuit, which, rubbed to powder, and mingled with water, was their constant food. The short time I continued in England, I made a considerable profit by showing my cattle to many persons of quality, and others: and before I began my second voyage, I sold them for six hundred pounds. Since my last return, I find the breed is considerably increased, especially the sheep; which I hope will prove much to the advantage of the woolen manufacture, by the fineness of the fleeces.

I stayed but two months with my wife and family; for my insatiable desire of seeing foreign countries would suffer me to continue no longer. I left fifteen hundred pounds with my wife, and fixed her in a good house at Redriff. My remaining stock I carried with me, part in money, and part in goods, in hopes to improve my fortunes. My eldest uncle John had left me an estate in land, near Epping, of about thirty pounds a year; and I had a long lease of the Black Bull in Fetter-Lane, which yielded me as much more; so that I was not in any danger of leaving my family upon the parish. My son Johnny, named so after his uncle, was at the Grammar School, and a towardly child. My daughter Betty (who is now well married, and has children) was then at her needle-work. I took leave of my wife, and boy and girl, with tears on both sides, and went on board the *Adventure*, a merchant-ship of three hundred tons, bound for Surat, Captain John Nicholas, of Liverpool, Commander. But my account of this voyage must be referred to the second part of my Travels.

Gulliver's Travels, ***by Jonathan Swift, first published in 1726, is divided into four books. The first, telling of the voyages to Lilliput and the second about Brobdingnab, the land of the giants, are the most popular.***

The Swiss Family Robinson

BY JOHANN WYSS

Illustrations by Lynd Ward

The shipwrecked Robinson family's adventures on a desert island have retained their fascination for several generations. After nearly ten years of peril and privation the Robinsons have succeeded in taming their wild home. Though boars and bears still rule much of the island, the family has built a fort, cultivated land, even domesticated animals. In this chapter the four boys decide to add a steed to their collection—not a horse, but an ostrich.

WE had been working very diligently. The bears' meat was smoked, the fat melted down and stored, and a large supply of bamboos collected. But I wished to make yet another excursion, and at early dawn I aroused the boys.

Fritz mounted the mule, I rode Lightfoot, Jack and Franz took their usual steeds, and, with the two dogs, we galloped off to try to capture one of the ostriches we had seen earlier.

Ernest watched us depart without the slightest look or sigh of regret, and returned to the tent to assist his mother and study his books.

Our steeds carried us down the Green Valley at a rapid rate, and we followed the direction we had pursued on our former expedition. We soon reached Turtle Marsh, and then, filling our water flasks, we arrived at the rising ground where Fritz discovered the mounted Arabs.

As Jack and Franz wanted a gallop, I allowed them to press forward. The two boys were still at some distance from us, when suddenly four magnificent ostriches rose from the sand where they had been sitting.

From *The Swiss Family Robinson*, by Johann Wyss.

Jack and Franz perceived them, and, with a great shout, drove them toward us. In front ran a splendid male bird, his feathers of shining black, and his great tail plume waving behind. Three females of an ashen-gray color followed him. They approached us with incredible swiftness, and were within gunshot before they perceived us. Fritz had had the forethought to bind up the beak of his eagle so that, should he bring down an ostrich, he might be unable to injure it.

He now threw up the falcon, which, towering upward, swooped down upon the head of the foremost bird, and so confused and alarmed him that he could not defend himself nor continue his flight. So greatly was his speed checked that Jack overtook him, and hurling his lasso, enfolded his wings and legs in its deadly coils and brought him to the ground. The other ostriches were almost out of sight, so, leaving them to their own devices, we leaped from our steeds and attempted to approach the captured bird. He struggled fearfully, and kicked with such violence, right and left, that I almost despaired of getting him home alive.

It occurred to me, however, that if we could cover his eyes, his fury might be subdued. I instantly acted upon this idea, and flung over his head my coat and hunting bag, which effectually shut out the light.

No sooner had I done this than his struggles ceased, and we were able to approach. We first secured round his body a broad strip of sealskin, on each side of which I fastened a stout piece of cord, that I might be able to lead him easily. Then, fastening another cord in a loop round his legs that he might be prevented from breaking into a gallop, we released him from the coils of the lasso.

"Do you know," said I to the boys, "how the natives of India secure a newly captured elephant?"

"Oh, yes!" said Fritz. "They fasten him between two tame elephants. We'll do that to this fine fellow, and tame him double quick."

"The only difficulty will be," remarked Jack, "that we have no tame ostriches. However, I daresay Storm and Grumble will have no objection to performing their part, and it will puzzle even this great monster to run away with them."

So we at once began operations. Storm and Grumble were led up on either side of the recumbent ostrich, and the cords secured to their girths. Jack and Franz, each armed with a stout whip, mounted their respective steeds, the wrappers were removed from the bird's eyes, and we stood by to watch what would next occur.

For some moments after the return of his sight he lay perfectly still, then he arose with a bound and, not aware of the cords which hampered him, attempted to dash forward. The thongs were stout, and he was brought to his knees. A fruitless struggle ensued, and then at length, seeming to accommodate himself to circumstances, he set off at a sharp trot, his guards making the air re-echo with their merry shouts. These cries stimulated the ostrich to yet further exertions, but he was at length brought to a stand by the determined refusal of his four-footed companions to continue such a race across loose sand.

The boys having enjoyed the long run, I told them to walk with the prisoner slowly home, while Fritz and I collected a supply of caoutchouc. We soon caught up our advance guard, and without incident reached our tent.

Astonishment and dismay were depicted on the face of the mother as we approached.

"My dear husband," she exclaimed, "do you think our provisions so abundant that you must scour the deserts to find some great beast to assist us to devour them. Oh! I do wish you would be content with the menagerie you have already collected, instead of bringing in a specimen of every beast you come across. And this is such a useless monster!"

"Useless! Mother," exclaimed Jack, "you would not say so had you seen him run. Why, he will be the fleetest courser in our stables. I am going to make a saddle and bridle for him, and in future he shall be my only steed. Then, as for his appetite, father declares it is most delicate, he only wants a little fruit and grass, and a few stones and tenpenny nails to help his digestion."

The way in which Jack assumed the proprietorship of our new prize seemed to strike his brothers as rather cool, and there was instantly a cry raised on the subject.

"Very well," said Jack, "let us each take possession of the part of the ostrich we captured. Your bird, Fritz, seized the head, keep that; father shall have the body, I'll have the legs, and Franz a couple of feathers from the tail."

"Come, come," said I, "I think that Jack has a very good right to the ostrich, seeing that he brought it to the ground, and if he succeeds in taming it and converting it into a saddle horse it shall be his. From this time, therefore, he is responsible for its training."

The day was now too far advanced to allow us to think of setting out for Rockburg, so we fastened up the ostrich between two trees, and devoted the remainder of the evening to making preparations for our departure.

At early dawn our picturesque caravan began moving homeward. The ostrich continued so refractory that we were obliged to make him again march between Storm and Grumble, and as these gallant steeds were thus employed, the cow was harnessed to the cart, laden with our treasures. Room was left in the cart for the mother, Jack and Franz mounted Storm and Grumble, I rode Lightfoot, and Fritz brought up the rear on Swift.

At the mouth of the Gap we called a halt, and replaced the cord the boys had strung with ostrich feathers by a stout palisade of bamboos.

When we reached the sugar-cane grove, we again stopped to collect the peccary hams we had left to be smoked; and my wife begged me to gather some seeds of an aromatic plant which grew in the neighborhood, and which had the scent of vanilla. I obtained a good supply, and we moved forward toward Woodlands, where we intended to rest for the night, after our long and fatiguing march.

Our tent was pitched, and on our beds of cotton we slept soundly.

Next morning early we examined our farmyard, which appeared in a most prosperous and flourishing condition. The sight of all these domestic animals made us long even more than ever for our home at Rockburg, and we determined to hasten thither with all possible speed.

The number of our pigs, goats, and poultry had greatly increased since we had last visited our colony; and some of these, two fine breeds of chickens especially, my wife wished to take back with her.

We found that the herd of antelopes, which Fritz and Jack had driven through the Gap, had taken up their abode in the neighborhood, and several times we saw the beautiful animals browsing among the trees.

While at the farm, we repaired both the animals' stalls and our dwelling room, that the former might be more secure against the attacks of wild beasts and the latter fitted for our accommodation when we should visit the spot.

Everything at length being satisfactorily arranged, we again retired to rest, and early next morning completed our journey to Rockburg.

By midday we were once more settled at home. Windows and doors were thrown open to admit fresh air; the animals established in their stalls; and the cart's miscellaneous cargo discharged and arranged.

As much time as I could spare I devoted to the ostrich, whom we fastened, for the present. between two bamboo posts in front of our dwelling.

Next morning Fritz and I went off in the boat, first to Whale Island, there to establish our colonists, the Angora rabbits, and then to Shark Island, where we placed the dainty little antelopes. Having made them happy with their liberty and abundance of food, we returned as quickly as possible to cure the bearskins and add the provisions we had brought to the stores lying in our cellar.

As we returned we caught up Jack, making his way in great glee toward Rockburg. He was carrying, in a basket, an immense eel, which he and Ernest had secured.

Ernest had set, on the previous night, a couple of lines. One had been dragged away, but on the other they found this splendid fellow.

It proved delicious. Half was prepared for dinner, and the other half salted and stowed away.

We now, for a short time, again turned our attention to our duties about the house.

Thinking that the veranda would be greatly improved by some creepers, I sowed, round the foot of each bamboo pillar, vanilla and pepper seed, as well as that of other creeping plants, which would not only give the house a pleasanter aspect but also afford us shade during the summer months.

I constructed a couple of hen coops too, for the hens and their

little chicks which we had brought from Woodlands, for I knew that if I left them unprotected, the inquisitive dispositions of Knips and Fangs might induce them to make anatomical experiments which would be detrimental to the welfare of the youngsters.

Ernest's ratskins were voted a nuisance within doors, and were tied together and hung up outside; so powerful was the odor they emitted that even then Jack would pretend to faint every time he passed near them.

The museum received its addition: the condor and vulture were placed there, to be stuffed when we should find time during the rainy season.

Having occupied two days in this way, we turned our attention to other duties: the cultivation of a wheat, barley, and maize field, and the taming of the captive.

As agriculture was, though the least to our taste, the most important of these several duties, we set about it first. The animals drew the plow, but the digging and hoeing taxed our powers of endurance to the utmost.

We worked two hours in the morning and two in the evening. Fully did we realize the words of Scripture: "In the sweat of thy face shalt thou eat bread."

In the interval we devoted our attention to the ostrich. But

our efforts on behalf of his education seemed all in vain. He appeared as untamable as ever. I determined, therefore, to adopt the plan which had subdued the refractory eagle.

The effect of the tobacco fumes almost alarmed me. The ostrich sank to the ground and lay motionless. Slowly, at length, he arose, and paced up and down between the bamboo posts.

He was subdued, but to my dismay resolutely refused all food. I feared he would die. For three days he pined, growing weaker each day.

"Food he must have!" said I to my wife. "Food he must have!" The mother determined to attempt an experiment. She prepared balls of maize flour, mixed with butter. One of these she placed within the bird's beak. He swallowed it, and stretched out his long neck, looking inquiringly for a second mouthful. A second, third, and fourth ball followed the first. His appetite returned, and his strength came again.

All the wild nature of the bird had gone, and I saw with delight that we might begin his education as soon as we chose. Rice, guavas, maize, and corn he ate readily—*washing it down,* as Jack expressed it, with small pebbles, to the great surprise of Franz, to whom I explained that the ostrich was merely following the instinct common to all birds; that he required these pebbles to digest his food, just as smaller birds require gravel.

After a month of careful training, our captive would trot, gallop, obey the sound of our voice, feed from our hand; and, in fact, showed himself perfectly docile. Now our ingenuity was taxed to the utmost. How were we to saddle and bridle a bird? First, for a bit for his beak. Vague ideas passed through my mind, but every one I was obliged to reject. A plan at length occurred to me. I recollected the effect of light and its absence upon the ostrich, how his movements were checked by sudden darkness, and how, with the light, power returned to his limbs.

I immediately constructed a leathern hood, to reach from the neck to the beak, cutting holes in it for the eyes and ears.

Over the eyeholes I contrived square flaps or blinkers, which were so arranged with whalebone springs that they closed tightly of themselves. The reins were connected with these blinkers, so that the flaps might be raised or allowed to close at the rider's pleasure.

When both blinkers were open, the ostrich would gallop straight ahead. Close his right eye and he turned to the left, close his left and he turned to the right, shut both and he stood stock-still.

I was justly proud of my contrivance, but, before I could really test its utility, I was obliged to make a saddle. After several failures, I succeeded in manufacturing one to my liking, and in properly securing it. It was something like an old-fashioned trooper's saddle, peaked before and behind—for my great fear was lest the boys should fall. This curious-looking contrivance I placed upon the shoulders as near the neck as possible, and secured it with strong girths round the wings and across the breast, to avoid all possibility of the saddle slipping down the bird's sloping back.

I soon saw that my plan would succeed, though skill and considerable practice were necessary in the use of my patent bridle. It was difficult to remember that to check the courser s speed it was necessary to slacken rein, and that the tighter the reins were drawn, the faster he would fly. We at length, however, all learned to manage Master Hurricane, and the distance between Rockburg and Falconhurst was traversed in an almost incredibly short space of time. The marvelous speed of the bird again revived the dispute as to the ownership, and I was obliged to interfere.

"Jack shall retain the ostrich," said I, "for it is most suited to him. He is a lighter weight than either of you his elder brothers, and Franz is not yet strong enough to manage such a fleet courser. But he is so far to be considered common property, that all may practice on him occasionally. And, in a case of necessity, anyone may mount him."

The Swiss Family Robinson *was first published in 1813.*

Friday's Rescue

BY DANIEL DEFOE

Illustrations by Lynd Ward

The story of Robinson Crusoe was undoubtedly suggested to Daniel Defoe by the true shipwreck experiences of Alexander Selkirk, who managed to keep himself alive on the island of Juan Fernandez for more than four years before he was rescued. However, Defoe's rich imagination supplied most of the vivid details of Crusoe's adventure, including the incident of how he acquired his "man Friday."

ABOUT a year and a half after I had entertained these notions, and by long musing had, as it were, resolved to put them into execution, I was surprised one morning early with seeing no less than five canoes all on shore together, on my side of the island, and the people who belonged to them all landed. The number of them broke all my measures, for seeing so many, and knowing that they aways came four, or sometimes more in a boat, I could not tell what to think of it, or how to take my measures to attack twenty or thirty men, single-handed, so I lay still in my castle, perplexed and discomforted. However, I put myself into all the same postures for an attack that I had formerly provided, and was just ready for action, if anything had presented. Having waited a good while, listening to hear if they made any noise, at length, being very impatient, I set my guns at the foot of my ladder, and clambered up to the top of the hill by my two stages, as usual, standing so, however, that my head did not appear above the hill; so that they could not perceive me by any means. I here observed, by the help of my perspective glass, that they were no less than thirty in

From *Robinson Crusoe*, by Daniel Defoe.

number, that they had a fire kindled, and that they had meat dressed; how they cooked it, that I knew not, or what it was; but they were all dancing, in I know not how many barbarous gestures and figures, round the fire.

While I was thus looking on them, I perceived, by my perspective glass, two miserable wretches dragged from the boats, where, it seems, they were laid by, and were now brought out for the slaughter. I perceived one of them immediately fall, being knocked down, I suppose, with a club, or wooden sword, for that was their way; and two or three others were at work, cutting him open for their cookery, while the other victim was left standing by himself till they should be ready for him. In that very moment, the poor wretch, seeing himself a little at liberty, nature inspired him with hopes of life, and he started away from them, and ran with incredible swiftness along the sands, directly towards me, I mean towards that part of the coast where my habitation was.

I was dreadfully frightened (that I must acknowledge) when I perceived him to run my way, and especially when, as I thought, I saw him pursued by the whole body; and I expected that part of my dream was coming to pass, and that he would take shelter in my grove; but I could not depend, by any means, upon my dream for the rest of it, namely, that the savages would not pursue him thither, and find him there. However, I kept my station, and my spirits began to recover when I found that there were not above three men that followed him; and still more was I encouraged, when I found that he outstripped them exceedingly in running, and gained ground of them, so that if he could but hold out for half an hour, I saw he would fairly get away from them all.

There was between them and my castle, the creek, which I mentioned often at the first part of my story, when I landed my cargoes out of the ship; and this I knew he must necessarily swim over, or the poor wretch would be taken there; but when the savage who was escaping came thither, he made nothing of it, though the tide was then up, but plunging in, he swam through it in about thirty strokes, or thereabouts, landed, and ran on with exceeding strength and swiftness. When the three pursuers came to the creek, I found that two of them could

swim, but the third could not, and that he, standing on the other side, looked at the others, but went no farther, and soon after went softly back again, which, as it happened, was very well for him.

I observed that the two who swam were yet twice as long swimming over the creek as the fellow was that fled from them. It came now very warmly upon my thoughts, and indeed irresistibly, that now was my time to get me a servant, and perhaps, a companion or assistant, and that I was called plainly by Providence to save this poor creature's life. I immediately got down the ladders, fetched my two guns, for they were both at the foot of the ladders, and getting up again with the same haste to the top of the hill, I crossed towards the sea; and, having a very short cut, and all down hill, clapped myself in the way between the pursuers and the pursued, hallooing aloud to him that fled, who, looking back, was at first as much frightened at me as at them; but I beckoned with my hand to him to come back, and, in the meantime, I slowly advanced towards the two that followed; then rushing at once upon the foremost, I knocked him down with the stock of my piece; I was loath to fire, because I would not have the rest to hear, though at that distance it would not have been easily heard, and being out of sight of the smoke, too, they would not have

known what to make of it. Having knocked this fellow down, the other who followed him, stopped, as if he had been frightened, and I advanced apace towards him; but as I came nearer, I perceived presently he had a bow and arrow, and was fitting it to shoot at me, so I was then necessitated to shoot at him first, which I did, and killed him at the first shot. The poor savage who fled, but had stopped, though he saw both his enemies fallen, and killed (as he thought), yet was so frightened with the noise and fire of my piece, that he stood stock-still, and neither came forward nor went backward, though he seemed rather inclined to fly still, than to come on. I hallooed again to him, and made signs to him to come forward, which he easily understood, and came a little way, then stopped again, and then a little farther, and stopped again; and then he stood trembling, as if he had been taken prisoner, and had just been to be killed, as his two enemies were. I beckoned to him again to come to me, and gave him all the signs of encouragement that I could think of; and he came nearer and nearer, kneeling down every ten or twelve steps, in token of acknowledgment for saving his life. I smiled at him, and looked pleasantly, and beckoned to him to come still nearer. At length he came close to me, and then he kneeled down again, kissed the ground, and, taking my foot, set it upon his head: this, it seems, was in token of swearing to be my slave forever. I took him up, and made much of him, and encouraged him all I could. But I perceived the savage whom I knocked down was not killed, but stunned with the blow, and began to come to himself. So I pointed to him, showing him the savage, that he was not dead; upon this he spoke some words to me, and though I could not understand them, yet I thought they were pleasant to hear, for they were the first sound of a man's voice that I had heard, my own excepted, for above five-and-twenty years. But there was no time for such reflections now. The savage who was knocked down recovered himself so far as to sit upon the ground, and I perceived that my savage began to be afraid; but when I saw that, I presented my other piece at the man, as if I would shoot him; upon this my savage, for so I call him now, made a motion to me to lend him my sword, which hung naked in a belt by my side; so I did. He no sooner had it than he ran to his enemy, and, at one blow, cut off his head so cleverly, no executioner in Germany could have done it sooner or better; which I thought very strange for one who, I had reason to believe, never saw a sword in his life before, except their own wooden swords. However, it seems, as I learned afterwards, they make their wooden

swords so sharp, so heavy, and the wood is so hard, that they will cut off heads and arms with them, and at one blow, too. When he had done this, he came laughing to me in sign of triumph, and brought me the sword again, and laid it down, with the head of the savage he had killed, just before me.

He was astonished how I had killed the other Indian so far off; and going to him, he stood like one amazed, looking at him, turning him, first on one side, then on the other; looked at the wound the bullet had made, which was in the breast, where it had made a hole, and no great quantity of blood had flowed, but he had bled inwardly, for he was quite dead. Then he took up his bows and arrows, and came back, and I beckoned for us to go away, making signs that more might come after them. Upon this, he signed to me, that he should bury them with sand, that they might not be seen by the rest, if they followed; so I made signs for him to do so; he fell to work, and had them both buried in the sand in about a quarter of an hour. I then called him away, and took him not to my castle, but my cave, on the farther part of the island; so I did not let my dream come to pass in that respect, namely, that he came into my grove for shelter. Here I gave him bread, and a bunch of raisins to eat, and a draught of water, which he was in great distress for, by his running; and having refreshed him, I made signs for him to go to sleep, pointing to a place where I had laid a great parcel of rice straw, and a blanket upon it, which I used to sleep upon myself sometimes; so the poor creature lay down, and went to sleep.

He was a comely handsome fellow, perfectly well made, tall, and well-shaped, and, as I reckon, about twenty-six years of age. He had a very good countenance, not a fierce and surly aspect, but seemed to have something very manly in his face, and yet he had all the sweetness and softness of an European in his countenance too, especially when he smiled. His hair was long and black, not curled like wool, his forehead very high and large, and a great vivacity and sparkling sharpness in his eyes. The color of his skin was not quite black, but very tawny, and yet not of an ugly, yellow, nauseous tawny, as the Brazilians, and Virginians, and other natives of America are, but of a bright kind of dun olive color that had in it something very agreeable, though not very easy to describe. His face was round and plump, his nose small, not flat like the negroes, a very good mouth, thin lips, and his teeth fine, well set, and white as ivory. After he had slumbered about half an hour, he waked, and came out of the cave to me, for I had been milking the goats in the inclosure just by. When he espied me, he came running, and laid himself on the ground again, with all the possible signs of an humble, thankful disposition, making many antic gestures to show it. At last he lays his head flat upon the ground, close to my foot, and sets my other foot upon his head, as he had done before, and after this, made all the signs to me of subjection, servitude, and submission imaginable, to let me know how much he would serve me as long as he lived. I understood him in many things, and let him know I was well pleased with him. In a little time I began to speak to him, and teach him to speak to me; and first, made him know his name should be Friday, which was the day I saved his life. I likewise taught him to say, "Master," and then let him know that was to be my name. I also taught him to say, "Yes," and "No," and to know the meaning of them. I gave him some milk in an earthen pot, and some bread, and let him see me drink some before him, and sop my bread in it, which he quickly imitated, and made signs that it was very good for him.

I kept there with him all that night; but as soon as it was day, I took him away with me. As we went by the place where he had buried the two men, he pointed exactly to the spot, and showed me the marks he had made to find them again, making signs to me that we should dig them up and eat them; at this I appeared very angry, expressed my abhorrence of it, made as if I would vomit at the thoughts of it, and beckoned with my hand to him to come away, which he immediately did, with great submission. I then led him to the top of the hill, to see if his enemies were gone, and pulling out my glass, I looked, and saw plainly the place where they had been, but no appearance of them or their canoes; so they were quite gone.

I then took my man Friday with me, giving him the sword in his hand, with the bow and arrows at his back, which I found he could use very dexterously, making him carry one gun for me, and I two for myself, and away we marched to the place where these creatures had been. When I came there, my very blood ran chill in my veins, and my heart sank within me at the horror of the spectacle. Indeed, it was a dreadful sight; the place was covered with human bones, the ground dyed with the blood, great pieces of flesh left here and there, half eaten, mangled, and scorched, and, in short, all the tokens of the triumphant feast they had been making there, after a victory over their enemies. I saw three skulls, five hands, and the bones of three or four legs and feet, and abundance of other parts of the bodies; and Friday, by his signs, made me understand that they brought over four prisoners to feast upon, that three of them were eaten, and that he, pointing to himself, was the fourth; that there had been a great battle between them and their next king, whose subjects it seems he had been one of, and that they had taken a great number of prisoners, all of which were carried to several places by those that had taken them in the fight, in order to feast upon them, as was done here by these wretches.

I caused Friday to gather all the bones and flesh that remained, and lay them together in a heap, and burn them to ashes. I found that he had still a hankering stomach after the flesh, and was still a cannibal in his nature, but I displayed such abhorrence at the very thoughts of it, that he durst not discover it; for I let him know that I would kill him if he offered it.

When we had done this, we came back to our castle, where I gave Friday first of all a pair of linen drawers, which I had out of the poor gunner's chest I found in the wreck, and which, with a little alteration, fitted him very well; then I made him a jerkin of goat's skin, as well as I was able; and I gave him a cap, which I had made of a hare's skin; and thus he was dressed, for the present, tolerably well; and mighty well was he pleased to see himself almost as well clothed as his master. He went awkwardly in these things at first; wearing the drawers was very awkward to him, and the sleeves of the jerkin galled his shoulders and the inside of his arms; but he soon got used to them.

The next day after I came home to my hut with him, I began to consider where I should lodge him; so I made a little tent for him in the vacant place between the two fortifications, in the inside of the last, and in the outside of the first; and as there was an entrance there into my cave, I made a formal framed door-case, and a door to it of boards, and set it up in the passage, a little within the entrance, and causing the door to open in the inside, I barred it up in the night, taking in my ladders, too; so that Friday could no way come at me in the inside of my innermost wall, without making so much noise in getting over, that it must needs awaken me, for my first wall had now a complete roof over it of long poles, covering all my tent, and leaning up to the side of the hill, which was again laid across with small sticks instead of laths, and then thatched over a great thickness with the rice straw, which was strong like reeds; and at the hole or place which was left to go in or out by the ladder, I had placed a kind of trap-door, which, if it had been attempted on the outside, would not have opened at all, but would have fallen down and made a great noise. I took care to take all the weapons into my side every night.

But I needed none of these precautions, for never was a more faithful, loving, sincere servant than Friday was to me; without passions, sullenness, or designs; his very affections were tied to me, like those of a child to its father, and, I dare say, he would have sacrificed his life for the saving of my own, upon any occasion whatever.

I was greatly delighted with him, and made it my business to teach him everything that was proper and useful, and especially to make him speak, and understand me when I spoke; and he was a very apt scholar, and he was so merry, so diligent, and so pleased when he could understand me, or make me understand him, that it was very pleasant for me to talk to him. And now my life began to be very easy and happy.

The Life and Strange Surprising Adventures of Robinson Crusoe, ***as Defoe called his novel, has an appeal that is as great today as when it was first published in 1719.***

Captains Courageous

BY RUDYARD KIPLING

Illustrations by Robert Reed Macguire

Harvey Cheyne, arrogant and pampered young son of an American millionaire, is washed overboard off the Newfoundland Banks straight into the arms of the rough crew of a fishing schooner. Unimpressed by his threats and boasts, the seamen do their best to make a real man out of Harvey.

THE weather door of the smoking-room had been left open to the North Atlantic fog, as the big liner rolled and lifted, whistling to warn the fishing-fleet.

"That Cheyne boy's the biggest nuisance aboard," said a man in a frieze overcoat, shutting the door with a bang. "He isn't wanted here. He's too fresh."

A white-haired German reached for a sandwich, and grunted between bites: "I know der breed. Ameriga is full of dot kind. I dell you you should imbort ropes' ends free under your dariff."

"Pshaw! There isn't any real harm to him. He's more to be pitied than anything," a man from New York drawled, as he lay at full length along the cushions under the wet skylight. "They've dragged him around from hotel to hotel ever since he was a kid. I was talking to his mother this morning. She's a lovely lady, but she don't pretend to manage him. He's going to Europe to finish his education."

"Education isn't begun yet." This was a Philadelphian, curled up in a corner. "That boy gets two hundred a month pocket-money, he told me. He isn't sixteen either."

"Railroads, his father, aind't it?" said the German.

"Yep. That and mines and lumber and shipping. Built one place at San Diego, the old man has; another at Los Angeles;

From *Captains Courageous*, by Rudyard Kipling.

owns half a dozen railroads, half the lumber on the Pacific slope, and lets his wife spend the money," the Philadelphian went on lazily. "The West don't suit her, she says. She just tracks around with the boy and her nerves, trying to find out what'll amuse him, I guess. Florida, Adirondacks, Lakewood, Hot Springs, New York, and round again. He isn't much more than a second-hand hotel clerk now. When he's finished in Europe he'll be a holy terror."

"What's the matter with the old man attending to him personally?" said a voice from the frieze ulster.

"Old man's piling up the rocks. 'Don't want to be disturbed, I guess. He'll find out his error a few years from now. Pity, because there's a heap of good in the boy if you could get at it."

"Mit a rope's end, mit a rope's end!" growled the German.

Once more the door banged, and a slight, slim-built boy perhaps fifteen years old, a half-smoked cigarette hanging from one corner of his mouth, leaned in over the high footway. His pasty yellow complexion did not show well on a person of his years, and his look was a mixture of irresolution, bravado, and very cheap smartness. He was dressed in a cherry-coloured blazer, knickerbockers, red stockings, and bicycle shoes, with a red

flannel cap at the back of the head. After whistling between his teeth, as he eyed the company, he said in a loud, high voice: "Say, it's thick outside. You can hear the fish-boats squawking all around us. Say, wouldn't it be great if we ran down one?"

"Shut the door, Harvey," said the New Yorker. "Shut the door and stay outside. You're not wanted here."

"Who'll stop me?" he answered deliberately. "Did you pay for my passage, Mister Martin? 'Guess I've as good right here as the next man."

He picked up some dice from a checker-board and began throwing, right hand against left.

"Say, gen'elmen, this is deader'n mud. Can't we make a game of poker between us?"

There was no answer, and he puffed his cigarette, swung his legs, and drummed on the table with rather dirty fingers. Then he pulled out a roll of bills as if to count them.

"How's your mamma this afternoon?" a man said. "I didn't see her at lunch."

"In her state-room, I guess. She's 'most always sick on the ocean. I'm going to give the stewardess fifteen dollars for looking after her. I don't go down more'n I can avoid. It makes me feel mysterious to pass that butler's pantry place. Say, this is the first time I've been on the ocean."

"Oh, don't apologise, Harvey."

"Who's apologising? This is the first time I've crossed the ocean, gen'elmen, and, except the first day, I haven't been sick one little bit. No, sir!" He brought down his fist with a triumphant bang, wetted his finger, and went on counting the bills.

"Oh, you're a high-grade machine, with the writing in plain sight," the Philadelphian yawned. "You'll blossom into a credit to your country if you don't take care."

"I know it. I'm an American—first, last, and all the time. I'll show 'em that when I strike Europe. Pff! My cig's out. I can't smoke the truck the steward sells. Any gen'elman got a real Turkish cig on him?"

The chief engineer entered for a moment, red, smiling, and wet. "Say, Mac," cried Harvey cheerfully, "how are we hitting it?"

"Vara much in the ordinary way," was the grave reply. "The

young are as polite as ever to their elders, an' their elders are e'en tryin' to appreciate it."

A low chuckle came from a corner. The German opened his cigar-case and handed a skinny black cigar to Harvey.

"Dot is der broper apparatus to smoke, my young friendt," he said. "You vill dry it? Yes? Den you vill be efer so happy."

Harvey lit the unlovely thing with a flourish: he felt that he was getting on in grown-up society.

"It would take more'n this to keel me over," he said, ignorant that he was lighting that terrible article, a "Wheeling stogie."

"Dot we shall bresently see," said the German. "Where are we now, Mr. Mactonal'?"

"Just there or thereabouts, Mr. Schaefer," said the engineer. "We'll be on the Grand Bank to-night; but in a general way o' speakin', we're all among the fishing-fleet now. We've shaved three dories an' near skelped the boom off a Frenchman since noon, an' that's close sailin', ye may say."

"You like my cigar, eh?" the German asked, for Harvey's eyes were full of tears.

"Fine, full flavour," he answered through shut teeth. "Guess we've slowed down a little, haven't we? I'll skip out and see what the log says."

"I might if I vhas you," said the German.

Harvey staggered over the wet decks to the nearest rail. He was very unhappy; but he saw the deck-steward lashing chairs together, and since he had boasted before the man that he was never sea-sick, his pride made him go aft to the second-saloon deck at the stern which was finished in a turtle-back. The deck was deserted, and he crawled to the extreme end of it near the flag-pole. There he doubled up in limp agony, for the "Wheeling stogie" joined with the surge and jar of the screw to sieve out his soul. His head swelled; sparks of fire danced before his eyes; his body seemed to lose weight, while his heels wavered in the breeze. He was fainting from sea-sickness, and a roll of the ship tilted him over the rail on to the smooth lip of the turtle-back. Then a low, gray mother-wave swung out of the fog, tucked Harvey under one arm, so to speak, and pulled him off and away to leeward; the great green closed over him, and he went quietly to sleep.

He was roused by the sound of a dinner-horn such as they used to blow at a summer-school he had once attended in the Adirondacks. Slowly he remembered that he was Harvey Cheyne, drowned and dead in mid-ocean, but was too weak to fit things together. A new smell filled his nostrils; wet and clammy chills ran down his back, and he was helplessly full of salt water. When he opened his eyes, he perceived that he was still on the top of the sea, for it was running round him in silver-coloured hills, and he was lying on a pile of half-dead fish, looking at a broad human back clothed in a blue jersey.

"It's no good," thought the boy. "I'm dead, sure enough, and this Thing is in charge."

He groaned, and the figure turned its head, showing a pair of little gold rings half hidden in curly black hair.

"Aha! You feel some pretty well now?" it said. "Lie still so; we trim better."

With a swift jerk he sculled the flickering boat head-on to a foamless sea that lifted her twenty full feet only to slide her into a glassy pit beyond. But this mountain-climbing did not interrupt blue-jersey's talk. "Fine good job, I say, that I catch you. Eh, wha-at? Better good job, I say, your boat not catch me. How you come to fall out?"

"I was sick," said Harvey; "sick, and couldn't help it."

"Just in time I blow my horn, and your boat she yaw a little. Then I see you come all down. Eh, wha-at? I think you are cut into baits by the screw, but you dreeft—dreeft to me, and I make a big fish of you. So you shall not die this time."

"Where am I?" said Harvey, who could not see that life was particularly safe where he lay.

"You are with me in the dory—Manuel my name, and I come from schooner 'We're Here' of Gloucester. I live to Gloucester. By and by we get supper. Eh, wha-at?"

He seemed to have two pairs of hands and a head of cast-iron, for, not content with blowing through a big conch-shell, he must needs stand up to it, swaying with the sway of the flat-bottomed dory, and send a grinding, thuttering shriek through the fog. How long this entertainment lasted, Harvey could not remember, for he lay back terrified at the sight of the smoking swells. He fancied he heard a gun and a horn and shouting.

RRM.

Something bigger than the dory, but quite as lively, loomed alongside. Several voices talked at once; he was dropped into a dark, heaving hole, where men in oilskins gave him a hot drink, and took off his clothes, and he fell asleep.

When he waked he listened for the first breakfast-bell on the steamer, wondering why his state-room had grown so small. Turning, he looked into a narrow, triangular cave, lit by a lamp hung against a huge square beam. A three-cornered table within arm's reach ran from the angle of the bows to the foremast. At the after end, behind a well-used Plymouth stove, sat a boy about his own age, with a flat, red face and a pair of twinkling gray eyes. He was dressed in a blue jersey and high rubber boots. Several pairs of the same sort of foot-wear, an old cap, and some worn-out woollen socks lay on the floor, and black and yellow oilskins swayed to and fro beside the bunks. The place was packed as full of smells as a bale is of cotton. The oilskins had a peculiarly thick flavour of their own which made a sort of background to the smells of fried fish, burnt grease, paint, pepper, and stale tobacco; but these, again, were all hooped together by one encircling smell of ship and salt water. Harvey saw with disgust that there were no sheets on his bed-place. He was lying on a piece of dingy ticking full of lumps and nubbles. Then, too, the boat's motion was not that of a steamer. She was neither sliding nor rolling, but rather wriggling herself about in a silly, aimless way, like a colt at the end of a halter. Water-noises ran close to his ear, and beams creaked and whined about him. All these things made him grunt despairingly and think of his mother.

"Feelin' better?" said the boy, with a grin. "Hev some coffee?" He brought a tin cup full and sweetened it with molasses.

"Isn't there milk?" said Harvey, looking round the dark double tier of bunks as if he expected to find a cow there.

"Well, no," said the boy. "Ner there ain't likely to be till 'baout mid-September. 'Tain't bad coffee. I made it."

Harvey drank in silence, and the boy handed him a plate full of pieces of crisp fried pork, which he ate ravenously.

"I've dried your clothes. Guess they've shrunk some," said the boy. "They ain't our style much—none of 'em. Twist round an' see ef you're hurt any."

Harvey stretched himself in every direction, but could not report any injuries.

"That's good," the boy said heartily. "Fix yerself an' go on deck. Dad wants to see you. I'm his son—Dan, they call me—an' I'm cook's helper an' everything else aboard that's too dirty for the men. There ain't no boy here 'cep' me sence Otto went overboard—an' he was only a Dutchy, an' twenty year old at that. How d'you come to fall off in a dead flat ca'am?"

" 'Twasn't a calm," said Harvey sulkily. "It was a gale, and I was sea-sick. Guess I must have rolled over the rail."

"There was a little common swell yes'day an' last night," said the boy. "But ef thet's your notion of a gale—" He whistled. "You'll know more 'fore you're through. Hurry! Dad's waitin'."

Like many other unfortunate young people, Harvey had never in all his life received a direct order—never, at least, without long, and sometimes tearful, explanations of the advantages of obedience and the reasons for the request. Mrs. Cheyne lived in fear of breaking his spirit, which, perhaps, was the reason that she herself walked on the edge of nervous prostration. He could not see why he should be expected to hurry for any man's pleasure, and said so. "Your dad can come down here if he's so anxious to talk to me. I want him to take me to New York right away. It'll pay him."

Dan opened his eyes, as the size and beauty of this joke dawned on him. "Say, dad," he shouted up the foc'sle hatch, "he says you kin slip down an' see him ef you're anxious that way. Hear, dad?"

The answer came back in the deepest voice Harvey had ever heard from a human chest: "Quit foolin', Dan, and send him to me."

Dan sniggered, and threw Harvey his warped bicycle shoes. There was something in the tones on the deck that made the boy dissemble his extreme rage and console himself with the thought of gradually unfolding the tale of his own and his father's wealth on the voyage home. This rescue would certainly make him a hero among his friends for life. He hoisted himself on deck up a perpendicular ladder, and stumbled aft, over a score of obstructions, to where a small, thick-set, clean-shaven man with gray eyebrows sat on a step that led up to the quarter-deck. The swell had passed in the night, leaving a long, oily sea, dotted round the horizon with the sails of a dozen fishing-boats. Between them lay little black specks, showing where the dories were out fishing. The schooner, with a triangular riding-sail on the mainmast, played easily at anchor, and except for the man by the cabin roof—"house," they call it—she was deserted.

"Mornin'—good afternoon, I should say. You've nigh slep' the clock around, young feller," was the greeting.

"Mornin'," said Harvey. He did not like being called "young feller"; and, as one rescued from drowning, expected sympathy. His mother suffered agonies whenever he got his feet wet, but this mariner did not seem excited.

"Naow let's hear all abaout it. It's quite providential, first an' last, fer all concerned. What might be your name? Where from (we mistrust it's Noo York), an' where baound (we mistrust it's Europe)?"

Harvey gave his name, the name of the steamer, and a short history of the accident, winding up with a demand to be taken back immediately to New York, where his father would pay anything any one chose to name.

"H'm," said the shaven man, quite unmoved by the end of Harvey's speech. "I can't say we think special of any man, or boy even, that falls overboard from that kind o' packet in a flat ca'am. Least of all when his excuse is thet he's sea-sick."

"Excuse!" cried Harvey. "D'you suppose I'd fall overboard into your dirty little boat for fun?"

"Not knowin' what your notions o' fun may be, I can't rightly say, young feller. But if I was you, I wouldn't call the boat which, under Providence, was the means o' savin' ye, names. In the first place, it's blame irreligious. In the second, it's annoyin' to my feelin's—an' I'm Disko Troop o' the 'We're Here' o' Gloucester, which you don't seem rightly to know."

"I don't know and I don't care," said Harvey. "I'm grateful enough for being saved and all that of course; but I want you to understand that the sooner you take me back to New York the better it'll pay you."

"Meanin'—haow?" Troop raised one shaggy eyebrow over a suspiciously mild blue eye.

"Dollars and cents," said Harvey, delighted to think that he was making an impression. "Cold dollars and cents." He thrust a hand into a pocket, and threw out his stomach a little, which was his way of being grand. "You've done the best day's work you ever did in your life when you pulled me in. I'm all the son Harvey Cheyne has."

"He's bin favoured," said Disko drily.

"And if you don't know who Harvey Cheyne is, you don't know much—that's all. Now turn her around and let's hurry."

Harvey had a notion that the greater part of America was filled with people discussing and envying his father's dollars.

"Mebbe I do, an' mebbe I don't. Take a reef in your stummick, young feller. It's full o' my vittles."

Harvey heard a chuckle from Dan, who was pretending to be busy by the stump-foremast, and the blood rushed to his face.

"We'll pay for that too," he said. "When do you suppose we shall get to New York?"

"I don't use Noo York any. Ner Boston. We may see Eastern Point abaout September, an' your pa—I'm real sorry I hain't heerd tell of him—may give me ten dollars efter all your talk. Then o' course he mayn't."

"Ten dollars! Why, see here, I—" Harvey dived into his pocket for the wad of bills. All he brought up was a soggy packet of cigarettes.

"Not lawful currency, an' bad for the lungs. Heave 'em overboard, young feller, an' try agin."

"It's been stole!" cried Harvey hotly.

"You'll hev to wait till you see your pa, to reward me, then?"

"A hundred and thirty-four dollars—all stolen," said Harvey, hunting wildly through his pocket. "Give them back."

A curious change flitted across old Troop's hard face. "What might you have been doin' at your time o' life with one hundred an' thirty-four dollars, young feller?"

"It was part of my pocket-money—for a month." This Harvey thought would be a knock-down blow, and it was—indirectly.

"Oh! One hundred and thirty-four dollars is only part of his pocket-money—for one month only! You don't remember hittin' anything when you fell over, do you? Crack agin a stanchion, le's say? Old man Hasken o' the 'East Wind' "—Troop seemed to be talking to himself—"he tripped on a hatch an' butted the mainmast with his head—hardish. 'Baout three weeks afterwards, old man Hasken he would hev it that the 'East Wind' was a commerce-destroyin' man-o'-war, an' so he declared war on Sable Island because it was Bridish, an' the shoals run aout too far. They sewed him up in a bed-bag, his head an' feet appearin', fer the rest o' the trip, an' now he's to home in Essex playin' with little rag dolls."

Harvey choked with rage, but Troop went on consolingly: "We're sorry fer you. We're very sorry fer you—an' so young. We won't say no more abaout the money, I guess."

" 'Course you won't. You stole it."

"Suit yourself. We stole it ef it's any comfort to you. Naow, abaout goin' back. Allowin' we could do it, which we can't, you ain't in no fit state to go back to your home, an' we've jest come on to the Banks workin' fer our bread. We don't see the ha'af of a hundred dollars a month, let alone pocket-money; an' with good luck we'll be ashore again somewheres abaout the first weeks o' September."

"But—but it's May now, and I can't stay here doin' nothing just because you want to fish. I can't, I tell you!"

"Right an' jest; jest an' right. No one asks you to do nothin'. There's a heap as you can do, for Otto he went overboard on Le Have. I mistrust he lost his grip in a gale we f'und there. Anyways he never come back to deny it. You've turned up, plain, plump providential for all concerned. I mistrust, though, there's ruther few things you kin do. Ain't thet so?"

"I can make it lively for you and your crowd when we get ashore," said Harvey, with a vicious nod, murmuring vague threats about "piracy," at which Troop almost—not quite—smiled.

"Excep' talk. I'd forgot that. You ain't asked to talk more'n you've a mind to aboard the 'We're Here.' Keep your eyes open, an' help Dan to do ez he's bid, an' sechlike, an' I'll give you—you ain't wuth it, but I'll give you—ten and a ha'af a month; say thirty-five at the end o' the trip. A little work will ease up your head, an' you kin tell us all abaout your dad an' your ma an' your money efterwards."

"She's on the steamer," said Harvey, his eyes filling with tears. "Take me to New York at once."

"Poor woman—poor woman! When she has you back she'll forgit it all, though. There's eight of us on the 'We're Here,' an' ef we went back naow—it's more'n a thousand mile—we'd lose the season. The men they wouldn't hev it—even allowin' I was agreeable."

"But my father would make it all right."

"He'd try. I don't doubt he'd try," said Troop, "but a whole season's catch is eight men's bread; an' you'll be better in your health when you see him in the fall. Go forward an' help Dan. It's ten an' a ha'af a month, ez I said, an', o' course, all f'und, same ez the rest o' us."

"Do you mean I'm to clean pots and pans and things?" said Harvey.

"An' other things. You've no call to shout, young feller."

"I won't! My father will give you enough to buy this dirty little fish-kettle"—Harvey stamped on the deck—"ten times over, if you take me to New York safe; and—and—you're ahead a hundred and thirty dollars by me, anyway."

"Ha-ow?" said Troop, the iron face darkening.

"How? You know how, well enough. On top of all that, you want me to do menial work"—Harvey was very proud of that adjective—"till the fall. I tell you I will not. You hear?"

Troop regarded the top of the mainmast with deep interest for a while, as Harvey harangued fiercely all around him.

"Hsh!" he said at last. "I'm figurin' out my responsibilities in my own mind. It's a matter o' jedgment."

Dan stole up and plucked Harvey by the elbow. "Don't go to tamperin' with dad any more," he pleaded. "You've called him a thief two or three times over, an' he don't take that from any livin' bein'."

"I won't!" Harvey almost shrieked, disregarding the advice, and still Troop meditated.

"Seems kinder unneighbourly," he said at last, his eye travelling down to Harvey. "I don't blame you, not a mite, young feller, nor you won't blame me when the bile's out o' your systim. Be sure you sense what I say? Ten an' a ha'af fer second boy on the schooner—an' all f'und—fer to teach you an' fer the sake o' your health. Yes or no?"

"No!" said Harvey. "Take me back to New York or I'll see you—"

He did not exactly remember what followed. He was lying in the scuppers, holding on to a nose that bled, while Troop looked down on him serenely.

"Dan," he said to his son, "I was sot agin this young feller when I first saw him, on account o' hasty jedgments. Never you be led astray by hasty jedgments, Dan. Naow I'm sorry for him, because he's clear distracted in his upper works. He ain't responsible fer the names he's give me, nor fer his other statements—nor fer jumpin' overboard, which I'm abaout ha'af convinced he did. You be gentle with him, Dan, 'r I'll give you twice what I've give him. Them hemmeridges clears the head. Let him sluice it off!"

Troop went down solemnly into the cabin, where he and the older men bunked, leaving Dan to comfort the luckless heir to thirty millions.

"I warned ye," said Dan, as the drops fell thick and fast on the dark, oiled planking. "Dad ain't noways hasty, but you fair earned it. Pshaw! there's no sense takin' on so." Harvey's shoulders were rising and falling in spasms of dry sobbing. "I know the feelin'. First time dad laid me out was the last—and that was my first trip. Makes ye feel sickish an' lonesome. I know."

"It does," moaned Harvey. "That man's either crazy or drunk, and—and I can't do anything."

"Don't say that to dad," whispered Dan. "He's set agin all liquor, an'—well, he told me you was the madman. What in creation made you call him a thief? He's my dad."

Harvey sat up, mopped his nose, and told the story of the missing wad of bills. "I'm not crazy," he wound up. "Only—your father has never seen more than a five-dollar bill at a time, and my father could buy up this boat once a week and never miss it."

"You don't know what the 'We're Here' 's worth. Your dad must hev a pile o' money. How did he git it? Dad sez loonies can't shake out a straight yarn. Go ahead."

"In gold mines and things, West."

"I've read o' that kind o' business. Out West, too? Does he go around with a pistol on a trick-pony, same ez the circus? They call that the Wild West, and I've heard that their spurs an' bridles was solid silver."

"You are a chump!" said Harvey, amused in spite of himself. "My father hasn't any use for ponies. When he wants to ride he takes his car."

"Haow? Lobster-car?"

"No. His own private car, of course. You've seen a private car some time in your life?"

"Slatin Beeman he hez one," said Dan cautiously. "I saw her at the Union Depot in Boston, with three niggers hoggin' her run." (Dan meant cleaning the windows.) "But Slatin Beeman he owns 'baout every railroad on Long Island, they say; an' they say he's bought 'baout ha'af Noo Hampshire an' run a line-fence around her, an' filled her up with lions an' tigers an' bears an' buffalo an' crocodiles an' such all. Slatin Beeman he's a millionaire. I've seen his car. Yes?"

"Well, my father's what they call a multi-millionaire; and he has two private cars. One's named for me, the 'Harvey,' and one for my mother, the 'Constance.'"

"Hold on," said Dan. "Dad don't ever let me swear, but I

guess you can. 'Fore we go ahead, I want you to say hope you may die if you're lying."

"Of course," said Harvey.

"Thet ain't 'nuff. Say, 'Hope I may die if I ain't speakin' truth.'"

"Hope I may die right here," said Harvey, "if every word I've spoken isn't the cold truth."

"Hundred an' thirty-four dollars an' all?" said Dan. "I heard ye talkin' to dad, an' I ha'af looked you'd be swallered up, same's Jonah."

Harvey protested himself red in the face. Dan was a shrewd young person along his own lines, and ten minutes' questioning convinced him that Harvey was not lying—much. Besides, he had bound himself by the most terrible oath known to boyhood, and yet he sat, alive, with a red-ended nose, in the scuppers, recounting marvels upon marvels.

"Gosh!" said Dan at last from the very bottom of his soul when Harvey had completed an inventory of the car named in his honour. Then a grin of mischievous delight overspread his broad face. "I believe you, Harvey. Dad's made a mistake fer once in his life."

"He has, sure," said Harvey, who was meditating an early revenge.

"He'll be mad clear through. Dad jest hates to be mistook in his jedgments." Dan lay back and slapped his thigh. "Oh, Harvey, don't you spile the catch by lettin' on."

"I don't want to be knocked down again. I'll get even with him, though."

"Never heard any man ever got even with dad. But he'd knock ye down again sure. The more he was mistook the more he'd do it. But, gold mines and pistols—"

"I never said a word about pistols," Harvey cut in, for he was on his oath.

"That's so; no more you did. Two private cars, then, one named fer you an' one fer her; an' two hundred dollars a month pocket-money, all knocked into the scuppers fer not workin' fer ten an' a ha'af a month! It's the top haul o' the season." He exploded with noiseless chuckles.

"Then I was right?" said Harvey, who thought he had found a sympathiser.

"You was wrong; the wrongest kind o' wrong! You take right hold an' pitch in 'longside o' me, or you'll catch it, an' I'll catch it fer backin' you up. Dad always gives me double helps 'cause I'm his son, an' he hates favourin' folk. Guess you're kinder mad at dad. I've been that way time an' again. But dad's a mighty jest man; all the fleet says so."

"Looks like justice, this, don't it?" Harvey pointed to his outraged nose.

"Thet's nothin'. Lets the shore blood outer you. Dad did it for yer health. Say, though, I can't have dealin's with a man that thinks me or dad or any one on the 'We're Here' 's a thief. We ain't any common wharf-end crowd by any manner o' means. We're fishermen, an' we've shipped together for six years an' more. Don't you make any mistake on that! I told ye dad don't let me swear. He calls 'em vain oaths, and pounds me; but ef I could say what you said 'baout your pap an' his fixin's, I'd say that 'baout your dollars. I dunno what was in your pockets when I dried your kit, fer I didn't look to see; but I'd say, using the very same words ez you used jest now, neither me nor dad—an' we was the only two that teched you after you was brought aboard—knows anythin' 'baout the money. Thet's my say. Naow?"

The blood-letting had certainly cleared Harvey's brain, and may be the loneliness of the sea had something to do with it. "That's all right," he said. Then he looked down confusedly. "Seems to me, that for a fellow just saved from drowning I haven't been over and above grateful, Dan."

"Well, you was shook up and silly," said Dan. "Anyway, there was only dad an' me aboard to see it. The cook he don't count."

"I might have thought about losing the bills that way," Harvey said half to himself, "instead of calling everybody in sight a thief. Where's your father?"

"In the cabin. What d'you want o' him again?"

"You'll see," said Harvey, and he stepped, rather groggily, for his head was still singing, to the cabin steps, where the little ship's clock hung in plain sight of the wheel. Troop in the chocolate-and-yellow-painted cabin was busy with a notebook and an enormous black pencil, which he sucked hard from time to time.

"I haven't acted quite right," said Harvey, surprised at his own meekness.

"What's wrong naow?" said the skipper. "Walked into Dan, hev ye?"

"No; it's about you."

"I'm here to listen."

"Well I—I'm here to take things back," said Harvey, very quickly. "When a man's saved from drowning—" he gulped.

"Ey? You'll make a man yet ef you go on this way."

"He oughtn't begin by calling people names."

"Jest an' right—right an' jest," said Troop, with the ghost of a dry smile.

"So I'm here to say I'm sorry." Another big gulp.

Troop heaved himself slowly off the locker he was sitting on and held out an eleven-inch hand. "I mistrusted 'twould do you sights o' good; an' this shows I weren't mistook in my jedgments." A smothered chuckle on deck caught his ear. "I am very seldom mistook in my jedgments." The eleven-inch hand closed on Harvey's, numbing it to the elbow. "We'll put a little more gristle to that 'fore we've done with you, young feller; an' I don't think any worse of ye fer anythin' thet's gone by. You wasn't fairly responsible. Go right abaout your business an' you won't take no hurt."

"You're white," said Dan, as Harvey regained the deck.

"I don't feel it," said he, flushed to the tips of his ears.

"I didn't mean that way. I heard what dad said. When dad allows he don't think the worse of any man, dad's give himself away. He hates to be mistook in his jedgments too. Ho! ho! Onct dad has a jedgment, he'd sooner dip his colours to the British than change it. I'm glad it's settled right eend up. Dad's right when he says he can't take you back. It's all the livin' we make here—fishin'. The men'll be back like sharks after a dead whale in ha'af an hour."

"What for?" said Harvey.

"Supper, o' course. Don't your stummick tell you? You've a heap to learn."

"Guess I have," said Harvey dolefully, looking at the tangle of ropes and blocks overhead.

"She's a daisy," said Dan enthusiastically, misunderstanding the look. "Wait till our mainsail's bent, an' she walks home with all her salt wet. There's some work first, though." He pointed down into the darkness of the open main-hatch between the two masts.

"What's that for? It's all empty," said Harvey.

"You an' me an' a few more hev got to fill it," said Dan. "That's where the fish goes."

"Alive?" said Harvey.

"Well, no. They're so's to be ruther dead—an' flat—an' salt. There's a hundred hogshead o' salt in the bins; an' we hain't more'n covered our dunnage to now."

"Where are the fish, though?"

"In the sea they say; in the boats we pray," said Dan, quoting a fisherman's proverb. "You come in last night with 'baout forty of 'em."

He pointed to a sort of wooden pen just in front of the quarter-deck.

"You an' me we'll sluice that out when they're through. 'Send we'll hev full pens to-night! I've seen her down ha'af a foot with fish waitin' to clean, an' we stood to the tables till we was splittin' ourselves instid o' them, we was so sleepy. Yes, they're comin' in naow." Dan looked over the low bulwarks at half a dozen dories rowing toward them over the shining, silky sea.

"I've never seen the sea from so low down," said Harvey. "It's fine."

The low sun made the water all purple and pinkish, with golden lights on the barrels of the long swells, and blue and green mackerel shades in the hollows. Each schooner in sight seemed to be pulling her dories towards her by invisible strings, and the little black figures in the tiny boats pulled like clockwork toys.

"They've struck on good," said Dan, between his half-shut eyes. "Manuel hain't room fer another fish. Low ez a lily-pad in still water, ain't he?"

"Which is Manuel? I don't see how you can tell 'em 'way off, as you do."

"Last boat to the south'ard. He f'und you last night," said Dan, pointing. "Manuel rows Portugoosey; ye can't mistake him. East o' him—he's a heap better'n he rows—is Pennsylvania. Loaded with saleratus, by the looks of him. East o' him—see how pretty they string out all along—with the humpy shoulders, is Long Jack. He's a Galway man inhabitin' South Boston, where they all live mostly, an' mostly them Galway men are good in a boat. North, away yonder—you'll hear him tune up in a minute—is Tom Platt. Man-o'-war's man he was on the old 'Ohio'—first of our navy, he says, to go araound the Horn. He never talks of much else, 'cept when he sings, but he has fair fishin' luck. There! What did I tell you?"

A melodious bellow stole across the water from the northern dory. Harvey heard something about somebody's hands and feet being cold, and then:—

"Bring forth the chart, the doleful chart,
See where them mountings meet!
The clouds are thick around their heads,
The mists around their feet."

"Full boat," said Dan with a chuckle. "If he gives us 'O Captain' it's toppin' full."

The bellow continued:—

"And naow to thee, O Capting,
Most earnestly I pray,
That they shall never bury me
In church or cloister gray."

"Double game for Tom Platt. He'll tell you all about the old 'Ohio' to-morrow. See that blue dory behind him? He's my uncle—dad's own brother—an' ef there's any bad luck loose on the Banks she'll fetch up agin Uncle Salters, sure. Look how tender he's rowin'. I'll lay my wage and share he's the only man stung up to-day—an' he's stung up good."

"What'll sting him?" said Harvey, getting interested.

"Strawberries, mostly. Punkins, sometimes, an' sometimes lemons an' cucumbers. Yes, he's stung up from his elbows down. That man's luck's perfectly paralysin'. Naow we'll take a-holt o' the tackles an' hist 'em in. Is it true what you told me jest now, that you never done a hand's turn o' work in all your born life? Must feel kinder awful, don't it?"

"I'm going to try to work anyway," Harvey replied stoutly. "Only it's all dead new."

"Lay a-holt o' that tackle, then. Behind ye!"

Harvey grabbed at a rope and long iron hook dangling from one of the stays of the mainmast, while Dan pulled down another that ran from something he called a "topping lift," as Manuel drew alongside in his loaded dory. The Portuguese smiled a brilliant smile that Harvey learned to know well later, and with a short-handled fork began to throw fish into the pen on deck. "Two hundred and thirty-one," he shouted.

"Give him the hook," said Dan, and Harvey ran it into Manuel's hands. He slipped it through a loop of rope at the dory's bow, caught Dan's tackle, hooked it to the stern-becket, and clambered into the schooner.

"Pull!" shouted Dan, and Harvey pulled, astonished to find how easily the dory rose.

"Hold on, she don't nest in the cross-trees!" Dan laughed; and Harvey held on, for the boat lay in the air above his head.

"Lower away," Dan shouted, and as Harvey lowered, Dan swayed the light boat with one hand till it landed softly just behind the mainmast. "They don't weigh nothin' empty. Thet was right smart fer a passenger. There's more trick to it in a sea-way."

"Ah ha! said Manuel, holding out a brown hand. "You are some pretty well now? This time last night the fish they fish for you. Now you fish for fish. Eh, wha-at?"

"I'm—I'm ever so grateful," Harvey stammered, and his unfortunate hand stole to his pocket once more, but he remembered that he had no money to offer. When he knew Manuel better the mere thought of the mistake he might have made would cover him with hot, uneasy blushes in his bunk.

"There is no to be thankful for to me!" said Manuel. "How shall I leave you dreeft, dreeft all around the Banks? Now you are a fisherman—eh, wha-at? Ouh! Auh!" He bent backward and forward stiffly from the hips to get the kinks out of himself. "I have not cleaned boat to-day. Too busy. They struck on queek. Danny, my son, clean for me."

Harvey moved forward at once. Here was something he could do for the man who had saved his life.

Dan threw him a swab, and he leaned over the dory, mopping up the slime, clumsily, but with great good-will. "Hike out the footboards; they slide in them grooves," said Dan. "Swab 'em an' lay 'em down. Never let a footboard jam. Ye may want her bad some day. Here's Long Jack."

A stream of glittering fish flew into the pen from a dory alongside.

"Manuel, you take the tackle. I'll fix the tables. Harvey, clear Manuel's boat. Long Jack's nestin' on the top of her."

Harvey looked up from his swabbing at the bottom of another dory just above his head.

"Jest like the Injian puzzle-boxes, ain't they?" said Dan, as the one boat dropped into the other.

"Takes to ut like a duck to water," said Long Jack, a grizzly-chinned, long-lipped Galway man, bending to and fro exactly as Manuel had done. Disko in the cabin growled up the hatchway, and they could hear him suck his pencil.

"Wan hunder an' forty-nine an' a half—bad luck to ye, Discobolus!" said Long Jack. "I'm murderin' meself to fill your pockuts. Slate ut for a bad catch. The Portugee has bate me."

Whack came another dory alongside, and more fish shot into the pen.

"Two hundred and three. Let's look at the passenger!" The

speaker was even larger than the Galway man, and his face was made curious by a purple cut running slantways from his left eye to the right corner of his mouth.

Not knowing what else to do, Harvey swabbed each dory as it came down, pulled out the footboards, and laid them in the bottom of the boat.

"He's caught on good," said the scarred man, who was Tom Platt, watching him critically. "There are two ways o' doin' everything. One's fisher-fashion—any end first an' a slippery hitch over all—an' the other's—"

"What we did on the old 'Ohio'!" Dan interrupted, brushing into the knot of men with a long board on legs. "Git out o' here, Tom Platt, an' leave me fix the tables."

He jammed one end of the board into two nicks in the bulwarks, kicked out the leg, and ducked just in time to avoid a swinging blow from the man-o'-war's man.

"An' they did that on the 'Ohio,' too, Danny. See?" said Tom Platt, laughing.

"Guess they was swivel-eyed, then, fer it didn't git home, and I know who'll find his boots on the main-truck ef he don't leave us alone. Haul ahead! I'm busy, can't ye see?"

"Danny, ye lie on the cable an' sleep all day," said Long Jack. "You're the hoight av impidence, an' I'm persuaded ye'll corrupt our supercargo in a week."

"His name's Harvey," said Dan, waving two strangely-shaped knives, "an' he'll be worth five of any Sou' Boston clam-digger 'fore long." He laid the knives tastefully on the table, cocked his head on one side, and admired the effect.

"I think it's forty-two," said a small voice over-side, and there was a roar of laughter as another voice answered, "Then my luck's turned fer onct, 'caze I'm forty-five, though I be stung outer all shape."

"Forty-two or forty-five. I've lost count," the small voice said.

"It's Penn an' Uncle Salters caountin' catch. This beats the circus any day," said Dan. "Jest look at 'em!"

"Come in—come in!" roared Long Jack. "It's wet out yondher, children."

"Forty-two, ye said." This was Uncle Salters.

"I'll count again, then," the voice replied meekly.

The two dories swung together and bunted into the schooner's side.

"Patience o' Jerusalem!" snapped Uncle Salters, backing water with a splash. "What possest a farmer like you to set foot in a boat beats me. You've nigh stove me all up."

"I am sorry, Mr. Salters. I came to sea on account of nervous dyspepsia. You advised me, I think."

"You an' your nervis dyspepsy be drowned in the Whalehole," roared Uncle Salters, a fat and tubby little man. "You're comin' down on me agin. Did ye say forty-two or forty-five?"

"I've forgotten, Mr. Salters. Let's count."

"Don't see as it could be forty-five. I'm forty-five," said Uncle Salters. "You count keerful, Penn."

Disko Troop came out of the cabin. "Salters, you pitch your fish in naow at once," he said in the tone of authority.

"Don't spile the catch, dad," Dan murmured. "Them two are on'y jest beginnin'."

"Mother av delight! He's forkin' them wan by wan," howled Long Jack, as Uncle Salters got to work laboriously; the little man in the other dory counting a line of notches on the gunwale.

"That was last week's catch," he said, looking up plaintively, his forefinger where he had left off.

Manuel nudged Dan, who darted to the aftertackle, and, leaning far over-side, slipped the hook into the stern rope as Manuel made her fast forward. The others pulled gallantly and swung the boat in—man, fish, and all.

"One, two, four—nine," said Tom Platt, counting with a practised eye. "Forty-seven. Penn, you're it!" Dan let the aftertackle run and slid him out of the stern on to the deck amid a torrent of his own fish.

"Hold on!" roared Uncle Salters, bobbing by the waist. "Hold on, I'm a bit mixed in my caount."

He had no time to protest, but was hove inboard and treated like "Pennsylvania."

"Forty-one," said Tom Platt. "Beat by a farmer, Salters. An' you sech a sailor, too!"

" 'Twern't fair caount," said he, stumbling out of the pen; "an' I'm stung up all to pieces."

His thick hands were puffy and mottled purply white.

"Some folks will find strawberry-bottom," said Dan, addressing the newly-risen moon, "ef they hev to dive fer it, seems to me."

"An' others," said Uncle Salters, "eats the fat o' the land in sloth, an' mocks their own blood-kin."

"Seat ye! seat ye!" a voice Harvey had not heard called from the foc'sle. Disko Troop, Tom Platt, Long Jack, and Salters went forward on the word. Little Penn bent above his square deep-sea reel, and the tangled cod-lines. Manuel lay down full length on the deck, and Dan dropped into the hold, where Harvey heard him banging casks with a hammer.

"Salt," he said, returning. "Soon as we're through supper we git to dressing-down. You'll pitch to dad. Tom Platt an' dad they stow together, an' you'll hear 'em arguin'. We're second ha'af, you an' me an' Manuel an' Penn—the youth an' beauty o' the boat."

"What's the good of that?" said Harvey. "I'm hungry."

"They'll be through in a minute. Snff! She smells good to-night. Dad ships a good cook ef he do suffer with his brother. It's a full catch to-day, ain't it?" He pointed at the pens piled high with cod. "What water did ye hev, Manuel?"

"Twenty-fife father," said the Portuguese sleepily. "They strike on good an' queek. Some day I show you, Harvey."

The moon was beginning to walk on the still sea before the elder men came aft. The cook had no need to cry "second half." Dan and Manuel were down the hatch and at table ere Tom Platt, last and most deliberate of the elders, had finished wiping his mouth with the back of his hand. Harvey followed Penn, and sat down before a tin pan of cods' tongues and sounds, mixed with scraps of pork and fried potato, a loaf of hot bread, and some black and powerful coffee. Hungry as they were, they waited while "Pennsylvania" solemnly asked a blessing. Then they stoked in silence till Dan drew breath over his tin cup and demanded of Harvey how he felt.

" 'Most full, but there's just room for another piece."

The cook was a huge jet-black Negro, and, unlike all the Negroes Harvey had met, did not talk, contenting himself with smiles and dumb-show invitations to eat more.

"See, Harvey," said Dan, rapping with his fork on the table, "it's jest as I said. The young an' handsome men—like me an' Pennsy an' you an' Manuel—we're second ha'af, an' we eats when the first ha'af are through. They're the old fish; and they're mean an' humpy, an' their stummicks has to be humoured; so they come first, which they don't deserve. Ain't that so, doctor?"

The cook nodded.

"Can't he talk?" said Harvey in a whisper.

" 'Nough to git along. Not much o' anything we know. His natural tongue's kinder curious. Comes from the innards of Cape Breton, he does, where the farmers speak home-made Scotch. Cape Breton's full o' niggers whose folk run in there durin' aour war, an' they talk like the farmers—all huffy-chuffy."

"That is not Scotch," said "Pennsylvania." "That is Gaelic. So I read in a book."

"Penn reads a heap. Most of what he says is so 'cep' when it comes to a caount o' fish—eh?"

"Does your father just let them say how many they've caught without checking them?" said Harvey.

"Why, yes. Where's the sense of a man lyin' fer a few old cod?"

"Was a man once lied for his catch," Manuel put in. "Lied every day. Fife, ten, twenty-fife more fish than come he say there was."

"Where was that?" said Dan. "None o' aour folk?"

"Frenchman of Anguille."

"Ah! Them West Shore Frenchmen don't caount anyway. Stands to reason they can't caount. Ef you run acrost any of their soft hooks, Harvey, you'll know why," said Dan, with an awful contempt.

"Always more and never less,
Every time we come to dress,"

Long Jack roared down the hatch, and the "second ha'af" scrambled up at once.

The shadow of the masts and rigging, with the never-furled riding-sail, rolled to and fro on the heaving deck in the moonlight, and the pile of fish by the stern shone like a dump of fluid silver. In the hold there were tramplings and rumblings where Disko Troop and Tom Platt moved among the salt-bins. Dan passed Harvey a pitchfork, and led him to the inboard end of the rough table, where Uncle Salters was drumming impatiently with a knife-haft. A tub of salt water lay at his feet.

"You pitch to dad an' Tom Platt down the hatch, an' take keer Uncle Salters don't cut yer eye out," said Dan, swinging himself into the hold. "I'll pass salt below."

Penn and Manuel stood knee-deep among cod in the pen, flourishing drawn knives. Long Jack, a basket at his feet and mittens on his hands, faced Uncle Salters at the table, and Harvey stared at the pitchfork and the tub.

"Hi!" shouted Manuel, stooping to the fish, and bringing one up with a finger under its gill and a finger in its eye. He laid it on the edge of the pen; the knife-blade glimmered with a sound of tearing, and the fish, slit from throat to vent, with a nick on either side of the neck, dropped at Long Jack's feet.

"Hi!" said Long Jack, with a scoop of his mittened hand. The cod's liver dropped in the basket. Another wrench and scoop sent the head and offal flying, and the empty fish slid across to Uncle Salters, who snorted fiercely. There was another sound of tearing, the backbone flew over the bulwarks, and the fish, headless, gutted, and open, splashed in the tub, sending the salt water into Harvey's astonished mouth. After the first yell, the men were silent. The cod moved along as though they were alive, and long ere Harvey had ceased wondering at the miraculous dexterity of it all, his tub was full.

"Pitch!" grunted Uncle Salters, without turning his head, and Harvey pitched the fish by twos and threes down the hatch.

"Hi! Pitch 'em bunchy," shouted Dan. "Don't scatter! Uncle Salters is the best splitter in the fleet. Watch him mind his book!"

Indeed, it looked a little as though the round uncle were cutting magazine pages against time. Manuel's body, cramped over from the hips, stayed like a statue; but his long arms grabbed the fish without ceasing. Little Penn toiled valiantly, but it was easy to see he was weak. Once or twice Manuel found time to help him without breaking the chain of supplies, and once Manuel howled because he had caught his finger in a Frenchman's hook. These hooks are made of soft metal to be re-bent after use; but the cod very often get away with them and are hooked again elsewhere; and that is one of the many reasons why Gloucester boats despise the Frenchmen.

Down below, the rasping sound of rough salt rubbed on rough flesh sounded like the whirring of a grindstone—a steady undertune to the "click-nick" of the knives in the pen, the wrench and schloop of torn heads, dropped livers, and flying offal; the "caraaah" of Uncle Salters's knife scooping away backbones; and the flap of wet, opened bodies falling into the tub.

At the end of an hour Harvey would have given the world to rest; for fresh, wet cod weigh more than you would think, and his back ached with the steady pitching. But he felt for the first time in his life that he was one of a working gang of men, took pride in the thought, and held on sullenly.

"Knife oh!" shouted Uncle Salters at last. Penn doubled up, gasping among the fish, Manuel bowed back and forth to supple himself, and Long Jack leaned over the bulwarks. The cook appeared, noiseless as a black shadow, collected a mass of backbones and heads, and retreated.

"Blood-ends for breakfast an' head-chowder," said Long Jack, smacking his lips.

"Knife oh!" repeated Uncle Salters, waving the flat, curved splitter's weapon.

"Look by your foot, Harve," cried Dan below.

Harvey saw half a dozen knives stuck in a cleat in the hatch combing. He dealt these around, taking over the dulled ones.

"Water!" said Disko Troop.

"Scuttle-butt's for'ard an' the dipper's alongside. Hurry, Harve," said Dan.

He was back in a minute with a big dipperful of stale brown water which tasted like nectar, and loosed the jaws of Disko and Tom Platt.

"These are cod," said Disko. "They ain't Damarskus figs, Tom Platt, nor yet silver bars. I've told you that every single time sence we've sailed together."

"A matter o' seven seasons," returned Tom Platt coolly. "Good stowin's good stowin' all the same, an' there's a right an' a wrong way o' stowin' ballast even. If you'd ever seen four hundred ton o' iron set into the—"

"Hi!" With a yell from Manuel the work began again, and never stopped till the pen was empty. The instant the last fish was down, Disko Troop rolled aft to the cabin with his brother; Manuel and Long Jack went forward; Tom Platt only waited long enough to slide home the hatch ere he too disappeared. In half a minute Harvey heard deep snores in the cabin, and he was staring blankly at Dan and Penn.

"I did a little better that time, Danny," said Penn, whose eyelids were heavy with sleep. "But I think it is my duty to help clean."

"Wouldn't hev your conscience fer a thousand quintal," said Dan. "Turn in, Penn. You've no call to do boys' work. Draw a bucket, Harvey. Oh, Penn, dump these in the gurry-butt 'fore you sleep. Kin you keep awake that long?"

Penn took up the heavy basket of fish-livers, emptied them into a cask with a hinged top lashed by the foc'sle; then he too dropped out of sight in the cabin.

"Boys clean up after dressin'-down, an' first watch in ca'am weather is boys' watch on the 'We're Here.' " Dan sluiced the pen energetically, unshipped the table, set it up to dry in the moonlight, ran the red knife-blades through a wad of oakum, and began to sharpen them on a tiny grindstone, as Harvey threw offal and backbones overboard under his direction.

At first splash a silvery-white ghost rose bolt upright from the oily water and sighed a weird whistling sigh. Harvey started back with a shout, but Dan only laughed. "Grampus," said he. "Beggin' fer fish-heads. They up-eend thet way when they're hungry. Breath on him like the doleful tombs, hain't he?" A horrible stench of decayed fish filled the air as the pillar of white sank, and the water bubbled oilily. "Hain't ye never seen a grampus up-eend before? You'll see 'em by hundreds 'fore ye're through. Say, it's good to hev a boy aboard again. Otto was too old, an' a Dutchy at that. Him an' me we fought considble. Wouldn't ha' keered fer thet ef he'd hed a Christian tongue in his head. Sleepy?"

"Dead sleepy," said Harvey, nodding forward.

"Mustn't sleep on watch. Rouse up an' see ef our anchor-light's bright an' shinin'. You're on watch now, Harve."

"Pshaw! What's to hurt us? Bright's day. Sn—orrr!"

"Jest when things happen, dad says. Fine weather's good sleepin', an' 'fore you know mebbe you're cut in two by a liner, an' seventeen brass-bound officers, all gen'elmen, lift their hand to it that your lights was aout an' there was a thick fog. Harve, I've kinder took to you, but ef you nod onct more I'll lay into you with a rope's end."

The moon, who sees many strange things on the Banks, looked down on a slim youth in knickerbockers and a red jersey, staggering around the cluttered decks of a seventy-ton schooner, while behind him, waving a knotted rope, walked, after the manner of an executioner, a boy who yawned and nodded between the blows he dealt.

The lashed wheel groaned and kicked softly, the riding-sail slatted a little in the shifts of the light wind, the windlass creaked, and the miserable procession continued. Harvey expostulated, threatened, whimpered, and at last wept outright, while Dan, the words clotting on his tongue, spoke of the beauty of watchfulness and slashed away with the rope's end, punishing the dories as often as he hit Harvey. At last the clock in the cabin struck ten, and upon the tenth stroke little Penn crept on deck. He found two boys in two tumbled heaps side by side on the main hatch, so deeply asleep that he actually rolled them to their berths.

Captains Courageous *was first published in 1897.*

ACKNOWLEDGMENTS

The publishers wish to express their appreciation to the publishers, agents, authors, and artists who have granted permission to use material appearing in this book.

Excerpt from *Call It Courage*, written and illustrated by Armstrong Sperry; reprinted in the British Commonwealth by permission of the Bodley Head Ltd. "The Devil Fish," from *20,000 Leagues Under the Sea*, by Jules Verne: illustrations by Kurt Wiese; reprinted by permission of The World Publishing Company, Cleveland and New York. "Gulliver's Voyage to Lilliput," from *Gulliver's Travels*, by Jonathan Swift, edited by Padraic Colum, copyright 1917 by The Macmillan Company, copyright 1945 by Padraic Colum and Willy Pogany; used by permission of The Macmillan Company. Excerpt from *The Swiss Family Robinson*, by Johann Wyss, and "Friday's Rescue," from *Robinson Crusoe*, by Daniel Defoe: illustrations by Lynd Ward, from the Illustrated Junior Library, published by Grosset & Dunlap, Inc.; illustrations reprinted by permission of Grosset & Dunlap, Inc. Excerpt from *Captains Courageous*, by Rudyard Kipling, reprinted by permission of Mrs. George Bambridge and Doubleday & Company, Inc.; reprinted in Canada by permission of Mrs. George Bambridge and The Macmillan Company of Canada, Ltd.